I.R.L.

JENNY
GOEBEL

Published in the UK by Scholastic, 2025
Scholastic, Bosworth Avenue, Warwick, CV34 6XZ
Scholastic Ireland, 89E Lagan Road, Dublin Industrial Estate,
Glasnevin, Dublin, D11 HP5F

SCHOLASTIC and associated logos are trademarks and/or
registered trademarks of Scholastic Inc.

Text © Jenny Goebel, 2025
Cover illustration by Omou Barry © Scholastic Inc., 2025
Supporting files © Shutterstock.com

First published in the US by Scholastic Press, an imprint of Scholastic Inc.,
Publishers since 1920. Scholastic, Scholastic Press, and associated logos
are trademarks and/or registered trademarks of Scholastic Inc.

ISBN 978 07023 4090 1

Printed in UK

Paper made from wood grown in sustainable forests
and other controlled sources.

MIX
Paper | Supporting
responsible forestry
FSC® C018072
FSC
www.fsc.org

1 3 5 7 9 10 8 6 4 2

www.scholastic.co.uk

TO MY LIFELONG FRIEND, JENNIFER,
AND MY GODDAUGHTERS
AVA AND GIANNA

CHAPTER 1

Please complete pages 45–49 of your mathematics workbook, which we shall review when in-person school resumes tomorrow. Sincere regards, Ms. Grant.

As I read my teacher's message in the chat, I held back a groan. I'd gotten used to Ms. Grant's formal way of speaking—*make that writing*. She never appeared on camera—she only communicated with her sixth-grade students through the chat function. Still, I knew she was watching and listening. And even if I'd gotten comfortable with her formal word usage, I'd never be comfortable with math homework.

"Tomorrow!" Mara blurted the second Ms. Grant logged off. "We'll finally get to meet you properly, Lucy. I look forward to it." I'd transferred to White Pine Secondary in the winter, when school was held virtually so no one had to navigate the treacherous rural Alaskan roads. Tomorrow was our first day of in-person learning, when I'd finally get to meet my new classmates in real life.

Mara's enthusiasm was enough to make me forget my homework for now. A grin spread across my face. "Me too!" My classmates looked and sounded way different from the kids back in San Francisco. I figured it was because they'd spent their entire lives in this tiny town. There was no movie theater, and until last year, the internet hadn't been strong enough for streaming. It made sense that the people in White Pine wouldn't know modern slang or talk about what was trending on social media. I'd even stopped following my favorite influencers. Now that I was living here, the latest TikTok challenges and dance moves didn't seem all that important.

"We haven't had a new student in eons," Mara continued. "Meeting you will be a treat for all of us."

Mara was clearly the unofficial leader of our class. She had glossy, straight auburn hair, and blue-gray eyes that felt penetrating even through the computer screen. To be honest, I'd found her intimidating at first—the snobby vibes she gave off made me want to curl up in a ball, or at least turn off my camera. She reminded me of Bailey Henderson, the girl who'd made my life miserable back in San Francisco. But despite Mara acting pretentious at times, she was really nice and had gone out of her way to make me feel welcome. All the students had, in fact. I just hoped they wouldn't change their minds once they met me in person.

"So how does everyone get to school? Do your parents drive you?" As the words bubbled out, I felt a twinge of pride for being brave enough to ask questions. I barely spoke at all during the second half of fifth grade. Not after I humiliated myself in front of everyone. Bailey had pretended to be my friend, then as a prank, she told me crazy hair day was on a day it wasn't. Everyone laughed, Bailey the loudest, when I showed up at school with pipe-cleaner curls and green hair a week early.

"*Drive us?*" Jamie said. A smirk was lingering on his face when I turned my attention back to my classmates. He was good-looking, wore his dark, medium-length hair slicked back, and oozed confidence. "Are you afraid of a little snow, Miss California?"

"Oh yeah, I'm terrified." Heat rose in my cheeks as I locked gazes with Jamie through the computer screen. Was this flirting? Was I, Lucy Bell-Rodriguez, actually flirting? With a real-life boy? Part of me wished Bailey were here to see this.

"We all walk. Or snowshoe," Josephine said, pulling me back from the brink of boy craziness. Really, she was doing me a favor. I didn't have to be in the same room as Jamie to know he was trouble.

"I can lend you an extra pair if you need them," Josephine

went on. Of all the students, she was the one I was most anxious to meet. She had a round, open face with large brown eyes and tendrils of curly hair framing her full cheeks. I'd spotted a sewing machine in the background of Josephine's screen a couple of weeks ago, but I hadn't yet gotten up the nerve to ask her about it.

I inherited my grandmother's sewing machine when she passed away a year ago. Before she died, I loved picking out bright, colorful fabrics and patterns with Grandma Bell, and then turning them into doll clothes, curtains, and pillows. I'd even sewn my own clothes for a while. That stopped when Bailey started making mean comments about my outfits. "Lucy's wearing one of her homemade dresses again. Doesn't she look precious?" she said right in front of a boy I liked. Then she pretended to whisper, "Doesn't your family have enough money to shop at, like, actual stores?"

White Pine was nothing like my old school, though, and Josephine was nothing like any of my previous classmates. I really hoped we could hang out in real life and work on sewing projects together. Maybe my parents were right after all. Maybe moving here was the fresh start we all needed. Still, I wanted to be cautious. I didn't want to get made fun of for dressing differently here, too.

"So, what's everyone wearing tomorrow?" I asked as breezily as I could. Mom had splurged and bought me a particularly

4

comfy pair of boots, ones with faux fur lining and silver laces, but I didn't know what to pair the boots with. I had no clue how people dressed here, considering I'd only ever seen the other students from the neck up. Did they follow trends, or did they dress more practically? If they all wore fleece-lined pants and turtleneck sweaters instead of crop tops and denim, that would be fine with me. Great, actually. I just wanted to know so I could pick something to blend in.

"Our school clothes, of course," Mara said, sounding surprised.

"Right!" I said quickly. I'd never owned designated school clothes. I'd always worn whatever I felt like, whether it was a weekend or any random Tuesday. This was a rural area, though. People did the types of things that caused more wear and tear on clothing. Maybe "school clothes" just meant stuff that didn't have holes or stains. But what if "school clothes" meant some sort of formal attire?

I furtively scanned the screen and found buttons and collars. Was Peter wearing a tie? My hoodie suddenly felt a little snug. I tugged it away from my neck. "And, um, what about backpacks? Kinda weird we haven't needed them all winter, right?"

Was it my imagination or were the other students exchanging puzzled looks? Had I said something embarrassing without realizing it? I'd been doing so well!

Finally, Josephine said, "I carry my lunch to school in a draw-string bag."

"Did you sew it yourself?" I asked excitedly.

Joshepine nodded and my heart soared. She did sew! That had to mean we were destined to be friends.

The school day ended, and we all signed off. But I was too excited about tomorrow to sit and relax. I didn't know what to do with myself and bounced from room to room. A snack in the kitchen. A few restless minutes trying to read in the den. Everywhere but into my parents' office. I didn't want to bug Mom and Dad, who were both working. We moved to White Pine so Mom could take a big, important job. Now that she was head scientist at the nearby research facility, she was always on the clock, even when she was home. Dad, on the other hand, was a small business owner and was forever putting in long hours.

I returned to my room and tried to work on my math home-work, but I just couldn't concentrate, so I took a break to heat up some frozen lasagna for dinner. After that, I still wasn't quite ready to face my math problems again. My room—the entire cabin, even—felt too small for my nervous energy. I had to get outside.

A blast of cold, crisp air hit me in the face as soon as I stepped out the front door. The sky was pitch-black. I wasn't sure I'd ever get used to the strange daylight hours in Alaska. It seemed like there was only ever too much light, or not enough. Now that it was technically spring, the sun lingered in the sky far longer. Somehow, that only made me miss it more after it went down.

I should've gone outside earlier. Nighttime in the middle of nowhere was intense. It was beautiful and isolated, but also a tad creepy. Not that city life hadn't been intense, too, just in a different way. The activity, traffic noise, countless structures, and hordes of people weren't nearly as overwhelming as not knowing what lurked in the trees and darkness. Even the silence was so absolute here that it seemed piercing.

I sucked in a large gulp of the frigid air and scanned a tangle of branches. I smiled at a sliver of the moon peeking out from behind a scraggly tree. The smile slid from my face, however, when a light flashed in the corner of my vision. When I turned my head to look for it, it was gone. It had to be my imagination. Still, a chill ran up my spine. It wasn't the first time I thought I'd seen a flicker in the forest that shouldn't be there.

I slipped back indoors. Even if I was a little spooked, the fresh air had done me some good. I was ready to tackle the last of my math homework.

I returned to my room thinking I'd knock out the remaining problems and then get to bed. My laptop was still on, but it must've gone into sleep mode. My screen saver was a photo of my best friend, Hana Lee, and me taken at the beach. The photo that was being displayed, though, was one I'd never seen before. It was an old black-and-white photo with a group of children standing on a porch. It must've been Halloween because the kids were wearing masks. Not latex masks or anything remotely realistic, though. Several had white sheets covering their faces, with cut-out eye and mouth holes. A few were wearing rough, ill-fitting clown masks. I thought they might be made of papiermâché. The kids looked so stiff and none of them were smiling.

I cringed, but it wasn't just the photo that made me uneasy. Mom and Dad were still in their office, and no one had been in my room. Why was this on my computer screen? I was standing there trying to puzzle it out when the speakers turned on for no reason. The sound of a woman crying filled my room. It was awful. She was sobbing so hard she was gasping for air. I lunged for my mouse pad. As soon as my fingers connected with it everything stopped. The woman's cries died out suddenly and my math problems—what I'd left on my screen before leaving my room—reappeared.

After that, I couldn't get the creepy photo or the audio to come back. It was like they were never there. The image wasn't stored anywhere on my computer, nor was a recording of a woman crying. I hadn't left a browser window open, so I didn't think it came from the internet, either. Had my laptop been hacked? Why would someone do something like that? Just to frighten me? It worked. I was completely freaked out. Even though it was over in a matter of seconds, and nothing else strange happened while I finished my homework, it took me a long time to fall asleep that night. Every time I closed my eyes, the children's masked faces flashed in my mind, and the woman's sobs rang in my ears.

CHAPTER 2

I snapped a picture of myself in the full-length mirror and immediately texted it to Hana. Then I quickly typed, *What do you think? Good first day fit?* With my dark gray jeans and a purple-and-green flannel, I'd gone for a look somewhere between casual and formal. I mean, my shirt did have a collar. That dressed it up some, didn't it?

I really wanted Hana to respond. And not just because I needed her reassurance about my outfit. It had been months since she'd responded to any of my texts. The radio silence didn't make sense. We'd been best friends for as long as I could remember. Then suddenly nothing.

To keep the blank screen from getting to me, I put my phone away. Then I shot a final glance at myself in the mirror before finding my way into the kitchen where Mom was grinding beans for her morning pot of coffee. She raised her eyebrows. "Didn't expect to see you up and ready this early. We'll leave in about forty-five minutes. I'll drop you off on my way to work."

I inhaled a deep breath, then let it out. I'd been rehearsing what I wanted to say in my head since I'd gotten up. "I was thinking . . . that since we live pretty close to the school, I can just walk there."

Mom didn't answer right away, and her dark brown eyes revealed nothing. Dad called it her "poker face," but personally, I thought "scientist face" was more fitting. Whenever she was presented with a dilemma, Mom calmly gathered information and then processed it before coming to any conclusions.

I waited patiently, knowing what would come next. The grilling.

"The roads are clear, but there's a solid snow base everywhere else," Mom pointed out.

"Snowshoes," I countered.

She nodded. "You'll be all alone."

"I navigated public transportation alone in San Francisco. How much harder can it be?"

"It's spring. The bears are starting to wake up."

"I'll carry bear spray." I could tell Mom still wasn't convinced. "You're always saying I need to get out in nature more. Here's my chance." That's when I flashed her my biggest, brightest smile, before adding, "Please? All the other kids walk to school. I want to start out on the right foot . . . or the right snowshoe."

And that, apparently, was the golden ticket.

Mom's calculating face broke into a smaller, more wistful smile than the one plastered on my face. "Okay, Luce, you win."

"Win what?" Dad asked groggily as he stepped into the kitchen. He'd fully embraced our new lifestyle and had stopped shaving the day we'd moved into the cabin. His new favorite dad joke was that he had more hair on his face than he'd had on his head in years.

"Our daughter has informed me that she'll be walking—make that snowshoeing—to and from White Pine Secondary today."

"Excellent decision!" he said. "The sun is out. It's going to be a killer day."

My parents met decades ago while surfing at Ocean Beach. Dad was the manager of a surf shop called Seas the Day, at the same time Mom was earning her PhD. Dad eventually bought out the shop owner and Mom became a leading expert in science and technology.

Dad still ran Seas the Day as an absentee owner. Which meant, most days, he worked from home in Bermuda shorts and a wool sweater. Meanwhile, Mom donned a lab coat and a name tag that read "Dr. Rodriguez" and commuted to and from the nearby research facility.

My eyes tended to glaze over when Mom talked about her job. It was all very experimental, but apparently in the world of renewable energy, there was something very special about White Pine, Alaska. So special that Dad gave up his beaches and I gave up Hana Lee and skate parks because we all knew this was the opportunity of a lifetime for Mom.

Mom filled a glass of orange juice for me while Dad ushered me to the table where a bagel and yogurt were waiting. "Eat up. Gonna need some fuel this morning," Dad said.

I'd barely finished my last bite when Mom whipped out her phone. "First-day photo time!" She actually dragged out the chalkboard she'd thrust upon me since kindergarten. On it the previous grade could be erased, and the current one could be written each year. In Dad's neat handwriting, it now read:

Lucy
Grade 6
Round 2

I groaned. "That makes it sound like I'm repeating sixth grade."

Mom cast an annoyed glance at my father. He shrugged. "What? I just meant round two of your first day. Should I change it?"

"No. Let's just get this over with," I said.

We moved outdoors so the glorious Alaskan wilderness could be featured in the background, and of course, Mom snapped way more photos than the situation called for. After that, my parents lingered while I strapped snowshoes on my feet, then found the address Mara emailed me and used it to pull up a GPS map on my phone. My parents both hugged me before I set off, and I made the mistake of glancing back at them after I'd gone a short distance. The looks on their faces—you'd think I was heading off to college.

As I went deeper into the woods, everything seemed so serene. The entire world was buffered by white. It was really peaceful, *at first*. There was soft pillowy snow piled on the ground and tree branches, and all that white glistened in the morning sunlight. It was starting to melt, though. Water was dripping all around the forest, from tree limbs and down the sides of charcoal-colored boulders. Wet snow was slushy and heavy. I'd snowshoed on ice-crusted snow and through powdery snow many times before but these conditions were the hardest.

I couldn't keep going full speed for long. The heavy snow was just too tiring. I'd worked up a sweat and when I stopped to rest, a cool breeze blew across the droplets on the back of my neck. I shivered. It was then that I noticed how eerily quiet it was. I shivered again, but this time it wasn't from the cold.

Movement in the forest caught my attention. I couldn't make out what it was, but there was something in a tree up ahead. The thought of a squirrel or a large bird was comforting for some reason—I guess the woods felt so empty that I was excited to see any sign of life. Anything to make me feel less alone.

I slowly made my way toward it. Whatever it was, I didn't want to scare it off before I got a good look. As I drew closer, I could make out the shape of wings and feathers. *Definitely a bird, then*, I thought . . . But there was something all wrong about its appearance.

It wasn't until I was directly below the branch where I'd first spotted movement that I understood what I was seeing. The bird wasn't perched on a limb and its wings weren't flapping. It was dangling and swaying as if from a noose. To my utter horror, I realized it was dead. The poor bird, a gull of some sort, had caught itself up in a fishing line. The line, which must've been wrapped around its neck and left wing and carried here from a different location, had tangled up and knotted itself to a tree branch. How long the bird must've fought against it, unable to fly away and search for food, I didn't know.

The sight of the gull's wasted carcass swinging in the wind made me feel sick to my stomach. I hated walking away, but there was nothing else I could do. The gull was too high in the tree, and the branches were too weak to hold me. Not only could

I not save the bird from this horrible fate, but I also couldn't do anything to free it in death, either.

A sense of dread came over me and I couldn't shake it as I continued making my way to school. What I didn't know then was that the gull was just a small taste of more frightening things to come.

CHAPTER 3

I didn't want to admit it, but I was starting to regret my decision to snowshoe to school. It was taking longer than I thought it would. Was I even on the right path?

I stopped to check the map on my phone. I was on the right track, but something felt off. Sure, the dead bird had left me rattled, but it was more than that. I felt like I was being watched. I felt a presence I couldn't explain. A presence that hadn't been there before. It was as if the forest had sprouted eyes. I patted my pocket to check for the bear spray. It was there. Really, though, I knew it wasn't a bear or any other creature, for that matter, that had me on edge. It wasn't a what. It was a who.

I clumsily spun in circles on my snowshoes. "Hello?" I called.

No one answered.

I stopped spinning and held very still. I listened for the snap of a branch, a whispered word, or a sigh. But, beside the drip,

drip, drip of the melting forest, the only noise I heard was my heartbeat drumming in my ears.

Still, I wasn't ready to dismiss my fears. My parents raised me to pay attention to my instincts. They said to remove myself from a situation if it felt wrong. This felt very wrong, but in all the scenarios I'd imagined escaping—a dark alley, an out-of-control party, an uncomfortable date—I never imagined myself deep in a forest and far from help. If I screamed, would anyone hear me?

I considered my options. I could turn around, but I was closer to the school than I was to home. Even if I contacted my parents, it would take longer for them to reach me than it would for me to find my way to safety. And if I called home in a state of distress, they might be less likely to let me venture out on my own next time. What if Josephine invited me over? If the kids here walked everywhere, I didn't want to be the only one getting dropped off every time I left my house. Plus, what if I was getting worked up for nothing? I'd been stuck at home for far too long. Small wonder that the outside world felt weird now.

With renewed determination, I started snowshoeing again. Of course, I steered clear of thick patches of trees and boulders—anything I thought a person or predator might hide behind. And the more time that passed without incident, the more I was able to relax. My heartbeat slowed. I hadn't realized how shallow my breaths had become, but my breathing returned to normal, too.

But my relief was short lived. I'd been wrong. I hadn't felt spooked because someone was watching me. No. I'd felt like something was off because things were too quiet. Too undisturbed. I glanced at the forest path stretching out in front of me. I knew I was close to White Pine Secondary now, but there wasn't a single footprint in the snow. *Why was that?*

The school had been closed all winter, but wouldn't someone have gone this way before I got here? My classmates said they were snowshoeing to school, too. And what about Ms. Grant, a parent, or a maintenance person? I was early, but not *that* early. I couldn't be the first to arrive.

The sense of dread that had lifted momentarily came crashing back. Had in-person learning been canceled? I sped down the path. I'd come this far. Even if the school was closed, I had to see for myself. I broke through the last patch of trees and skidded to a stop when I saw the building that awaited me in the clearing.

When the initial shock wore off, I fumbled for my phone and stared at the map. I was at the right place. At least, I was at the destination I'd set out for. But this couldn't be it. I mean, there was a sign in front of the building that read WHITE PINE SEC- ONDARY SCHOOL. But it was crooked and hanging from a single nail. The faded paint was hardly legible. The sign was creepy enough, but the sight of the actual school building made my heart plummet. It was clearly abandoned and had been for some time. Water was dripping in through a gaping hole in the roof, and the brick walls were black with mold, or were they charred? I couldn't tell.

There had to be some reasonable explanation. There always was, right? I reminded myself that I was the daughter of a scientist. I, too, could calmly gather information and then process it before jumping to conclusions.

Whatever happened to the school, it had happened years ago. It must have been rebuilt at a different location. Remote areas took longer to update in Google, didn't they? Maybe really remote areas took decades.

What I needed to do was find the new location. This was frustrating, but it wasn't the end of the world. I still didn't want to call my parents, but if I was going to arrive at the school anywhere near on time, I would need a ride. I closed the map on my phone and opened the contact list, then scrolled to my dad's number and hit call. When I placed the phone against my ear, it didn't ring. *Great.* No service.

I inhaled a breath of cold air, then let it out. Still not the end of the world. I just had to find a place where I could get a call to go through.

That was when it started to snow.

At first, it was just a few white, fluffy snowflakes—soft and pretty—but soon the flakes were coming at such a rapid pace that they blotted out my surroundings. So much for Dad's killer day.

I didn't feel confident I could find my way home in the storm and I didn't want to wander around looking for a signal in the falling snow. I'd heard stories before moving here—stories about people getting lost in blizzards and never coming back. Plus, I was hardly prepared to weather a storm. For one thing, I'd worn jeans. For another, I'd packed my school stuff, not survival gear.

Snowflakes bunched on my eyelashes as I eyed the ruins. I absolutely did not want to go inside. The roof looked like it could collapse any second, and who knew what I might find in there? Voles and other rodents? Would something larger have taken up residence for the winter? But . . . my jeans were starting to dampen in the snow. I shivered. I couldn't stay out in this much longer. I had to take shelter.

As much as I didn't want to go inside, I gathered my courage and walked through the gaping hole that had once been the doorway. The interior was in worse condition than the exterior. There were bars across the windows, surrounded by shards of broken glass. Snow had forced its way in through the cavities and crevices and blanketed areas in white. It must've been a fire

21

that caused all the destruction because everywhere I went, my snowshoes churned up ash and blackened the snow.

It was like walking through the skeleton of a giant beast. The blood and flesh were gone. All that remained were the bones.

I was careful to avoid the piles of rubble. If I didn't bother any critters that might be skulking, then they wouldn't bother me. Right? Still, I couldn't help but look around a little. As I made my way toward one of the corners, I discovered a few items that appeared to have been placed here after the fire. They weren't blackened and marred like everything else. I crept closer to get a better look. There was a teddy bear with a missing button eye, a thimble, an antique hand mirror with a sterling-silver frame, and a scroll. They were stacked together like some sort of shrine. I picked up the teddy bear first and gently gave it a squeeze. It was grimy and cold, but still soft. Then I dipped my index finger into the thimble. It was even colder. Next, I carefully unrolled the brittle scroll and read what was written in black ink:

Rest in Peace Our Beloved Angel

I gasped and let the parchment paper slip from my trembling fingertips. This was a memorial. *For a child.* The old school building hadn't just burned down—a child, or maybe multiple children, had lost their lives here.

My gaze darted around the building. It was so gray and frigid now; it was hard to imagine the heat of fire and the glow of a burning blaze. How awful it must've been to be trapped inside while the building was engulfed by flames. I felt a twinge of remorse for having disturbed the memorial. It seemed important to put it back exactly like it was. I righted the teddy bear and rerolled the parchment paper.

It was then that I caught my reflection in the hand mirror, but the image wasn't right. It was me, but it didn't look like me. I curled my fingers around the sterling-silver handle and drew it closer to my face. As I studied myself in the mirror, my blood turned to ice in my veins. Instead of loose strands of hair flowing from under my beanie, my hair was pulled into braids, and instead of my winter coat, I was wearing a floral cotton dress with buttons down the front and a lacy collar. I blinked once and the image shimmered away. In an instant my reflection was back to normal.

I dropped the mirror and didn't stick around to see where it landed. My heart pounded against my rib cage as I darted toward the gaping hole at the front of the building. It felt like the walls were closing in on me and I couldn't move fast enough in my clunky snowshoes. By the time I made it out of the ruins and back into the storm, my chest was tight, and I was breathing heavily. My jeans were still damp from before and the storm hadn't eased up, but I didn't care anymore. All I cared about was getting home.

Frantically scanning the ground, I could barely make out my tracks. The indentations were beginning to fill in with fresh snow, but they were there—shallow, elongated holes where my snowshoes had dug in. Step by step, I retraced my route. When I passed the swinging gull, I didn't look. Not that I could make out much more than a shadow in the flying snow. Everything beyond a few feet blurred into white. I panicked when a gust of wind completely erased my path, but then I caught sight of it again a moment later.

When the cabin finally came into view, my jeans were stiff and frozen. They felt like ice against my skin. I was shivering uncontrollably as I stripped off my snowshoes before pushing open the front door. But even then, I didn't feel safe.

I couldn't explain it, but it felt like something from the ruins had followed me home.

CHAPTER 4

I flung off my coat, beanie, and boots. Water pooled beneath them in the entryway. Then I ran to my room to change out of my soaked jeans. The ice on the denim had melted but my fingers were still numb. I fumbled with the button and zipper. Once I managed to replace the jeans with dry sweatpants, I retrieved my laptop. However, I was still shaking so badly, I could hardly type the right keys. It couldn't wait until I was less freaked out, though. For my own sake, I had to make sense of what was going on as soon as possible. Had I gotten lost? What happened to White Pine Secondary? Had my reflection really been different in the hand mirror, or was I just so upset by the memorial that my mind played tricks on me?

When I opened the email Mara had sent with the school address, I found that it was the same one I'd punched into my navigation app before setting out. I hadn't made a mistake.

Then I tried searching the school's website for an address even though I'd looked before. The contact page had a single, generic email address: the one my parents had used to register me as a new student. The bare-bones site hadn't seemed all that strange when we'd first discovered it. An elaborate website seemed like too much to expect from a tiny community. It hadn't occurred to us then that a physical address wasn't listed. There still wasn't one now.

Considering I'd gone to where Mara had sent me, did that mean it was all a prank? Had Mara sent me to the ruins on purpose? Were the other students in on it?

Despite the cold, my cheeks burned with shame and hurt. This wasn't the first time I'd been the victim of cruel jokes. Fifth grade had been brutal. But I thought my new classmates were different. They seemed so excited to meet me. I really thought we could be friends.

Now Mara and the others were probably all at the real school, talking about how funny it was that they'd sent me to the ruins instead. They'd probably laugh even harder if they knew how utterly spooked I'd been. That weirdness with the mirror . . . being so scared had really messed with my head. Just as I was thinking about how I NEVER wanted the other students to know I'd fallen for their prank, a new email popped up in my inbox. I clicked on it at once. It was a notice of early release from White Pine Secondary. Due to the unexpected weather, the students had been dismissed from in-person learning and afternoon classes were resuming online. At the bottom was a link to join.

My stomach did a somersault. The weather was terrible, and it had changed so suddenly. I shouldn't have been surprised that the students were sent home. But I wasn't ready to face them so soon, even if it was just online. If I didn't join, though, they would know how much they'd gotten to me. While my finger was lingering over the mouse pad, someone knocked on my door. I jolted upright, then relaxed when I heard my dad's voice.

"Lucy? Everything okay? Why are you home so early?"

I used my hands to brush loose hair strands back from my face, and then took a deep breath. "Yeah, um, it's just the weather," I yelled back. "Early release. I'm about to sign on to remote classes." Somehow, I managed to keep my voice steady so he wouldn't know I was upset. If he knew I was being bullied again, he'd be worried. It was hard enough running a business from thousands of miles away. I didn't want my problems to add to his.

"Right on," Dad said. "Let me know if you need anything."

"Sure thing," I answered as brightly as I could before turning my attention back to the link. My finger was still lingering over the mouse pad, and that's where it stayed while I summoned the courage to click on the link. Would the other students burst into laughter as soon as they saw my face? What if they'd somehow been watching me the whole time? Had they been hiding out in the woods, giggling at my confusion, and then my terror?

When Bailey had pranked me, I dissolved into tears and ran out of the classroom. I called my parents to pick me up, and I'd regretted it ever since. What I should've done was walk in with my head of pipe-cleaner curls and green hair held high, and act like it was no big deal. Instead, Baily had the satisfaction of watching me fall to pieces.

I didn't want to give Mara the same satisfaction I'd given Bailey. I didn't want my new classmates to know just how badly their little prank had rattled me. If I didn't sign on, they'd know they'd scared me out of my mind. And so, it was my pride that finally pushed me to log in.

When the boxes popped up, I expected to find smug and sneering faces staring back at me. They weren't, though, and there was no laughter, either. Instead, they were smiling and acting as if nothing strange had occurred.

"Hi, Lucy," Josephine said warmly. "We missed you this morning, but it's understandable that you wouldn't want to venture out, considering the storm."

I frowned at the screen. Was it possible that Josephine wasn't in on the joke? Either way, I was sick of this game. I couldn't pretend nothing had happened. Eventually I would need the correct school address, which meant my only option was to confront Mara. I might as well get it over with.

I jutted my chin and acted braver than I felt. "Why did you send me to the wrong address?" I asked, glaring directly at Mara.

Mara recoiled. "Good heavens. What do you mean?"

Maybe if we'd been in person, I might've been able to tell if she was faking innocence. Online, it was impossible. "The address you gave me for the school was for a burnt down building in the middle of the woods."

"What? Oh no." Mara's hands shot to cover her face. She groaned. "I didn't."

"You didn't what?"

"I was in a hurry when I sent you that. I don't have the school address memorized and I cut and pasted it from a source on the internet. I should've been more careful. I'm so sorry."

For a moment, I said nothing. Was it possible that it really was just a misunderstanding? Despite everything, I wanted to believe that my new classmates would truly welcome me into their group. I wanted to believe that they hadn't meant to prank me.

"The storm is dying down already," Mara said. "It doesn't appear there will be much accumulation after all. We'll most likely return to the school building for classes tomorrow and

I can assure you, the new building is quite close to the ruins. You were almost there, but I'll text you a link to the map this time, so you don't get lost again. All right?"

I gnawed on my bottom lip. The chat box was blank. Apparently, Ms. Grant was letting us sort this one out on our own.

What other choice did I have? Mara seemed sincere, and I didn't want to make a big fuss and tell them how horrible it had been. Really, I just wanted to move past this. They were being kind to me now and I didn't want to ruin it by holding on to my hurt and fears. "Okay," I said at last. "Thanks."

I should've been relieved, and for the most part, I did feel better. But, still, I couldn't entirely get rid of the unease that had settled somewhere deep inside my stomach. Maybe feeling this way was normal after what I'd been through at the ruins. Following a winter of isolation, though, my gauge for what was and wasn't normal appeared to be broken.

CHAPTER 5

Even though I was 100 percent sure I set my phone alarm before going to sleep, it didn't go off the next morning. What woke me was the sound of my sewing machine, whirring beneath its cover. I hadn't sewn anything for days, so there was no reason for it to be on. I sprang from bed and hit the off switch, but it kept making a *ch ch ch ch ch* sound, like a quiet train. It wasn't until I yanked the cord from the wall that it stopped.

When I glanced at the time on my clock, I nearly died. I only had ten minutes to get ready for school. I was over choosing my first day outfit, round two (or round three, by Dad's count). So, I threw on some long underwear under quick-dry joggers and a hoodie, ran to the bathroom, brushed my teeth and hair, scurried to the kitchen where I grabbed a granola bar from the cabinet and my lunch out of the fridge, then darted for the front door.

"Whoa! Slow down," Mom said as I blew past her.

"No time! Gotta go. I'm gonna be late."

She planted a kiss on my head anyway as I pulled on my winter coat and boots, which were exactly where I'd flung them when I'd been so rattled.

"Have a good day, honey!" Mom said.

"Bye, kiddo!" Dad yelled from somewhere down the hall. "Be safe!"

My stomach roiled with apprehension. "I'll try," I said.

It wasn't until I was out the front door that I remembered I still didn't know where I was going. I retrieved my phone and checked my text messages. Nothing from Mara. As if I needed anything else to unnerve me. I was about to text her when a message popped up on my screen. No words, just a link for a map. Why did she have to wait until the last possible moment to send it? Was she trying to stress me out? I swallowed my annoyance, typed *thanks*, hit send, and then clicked on the link.

Mara said the new school building was very close to the one that had burned down, but I still hated going down the same path that had caused me so much trauma the day before. I kept my eyes glued to the ground when I snowshoed past the dangling gull. The fresh snow had frozen over the night before and left a crust, which made for easier travel. It was a clear morning, and I was making good time. But when the charred brick walls and sunken roof came into view, I stopped. I checked the map, hoping it would divert me around the ruins. Weirdly, the blue line on the screen, the one I was supposed to be following, was bouncing all over the place.

I had lost cell service here before . . . My heartbeat quickened. I'd been so rushed that I hadn't had time to investigate where the new map led before setting off. Where was I supposed to go from here? The red marker stopped moving and appeared to indicate that my route ended at the ruins. I took a deep breath to stave off the anxiety building in my chest. A little technical difficulty didn't mean Mara had given me the wrong address again.

I held my phone up, trying to find a signal, and took a few steps forward. The lines on the map stopped shifting and the red marker stabilized on a point clearly beyond where I was now. That was the good news. The bad news was that I would have to walk right past the ruins again.

I kept my gaze on a thicket of trees ahead as I carried on my way. Still, I couldn't help but feel creeped out as I drew close to the old school. Now that I knew about the memorial inside, it seemed more like a tomb than a falling-down building. Even the air seemed colder as I worked my way through the snow and around a blackened brick wall.

When I was a good five or ten feet beyond the ruins, I thought

I was past the hard part. I was ready to meet my classmates at last and fully expected to find the new school building just beyond the last clump of trees. However, when I broke through the last of the branches blocking my view, it wasn't another building I found. It was a tiny cemetery with snow-dusted head-stones. My breath caught in my throat. In a daze, I headed to the nearest grave marker and removed my right glove. With my bare hand, I brushed fresh, new flakes away from the cold, hard granite.

Jamie Gregson
1913–1925

That was odd. Gregson was my classmate Jamie's last name. Maybe this grave belonged to Jamie's father? Except that the dates carved into the stone made it clear that this Jamie Gregson had passed long before the Jamie I knew came into this world. My Jamie must've been named after an ancestor who lived generations before.

I stumbled to the next marker and wiped it clear with much less delicacy than I had the last.

The blood drained from my face. My fingers and toes tingled, and I felt lightheaded. Staring at the letters and numbers carved into the stone, I read the epitaph over and over.

Mara Foster
1912–1925

I gasped. One headstone could be dismissed as a coincidence, but two? Clinging to a shred of hope that this wasn't what it seemed, I dusted off each of the remaining headstones. In the end, there were three neat rows of markers, four in each row. Twelve in total—one with a name carved on it for each member of my class.

Memories came flooding back like pieces of a puzzle—the weird questions about my life in San Francisco, their odd clothing . . . now that I thought about it, the little I'd seen of their on-camera bedrooms had been noticeably outdated. Who kept a gas lantern hanging by their bed these days? Mara. That was who. Mara, whose grave marker read 1912–1925. Mara, who had lived and *died* over a century ago. If the headstones were to be believed, all my new classmates had been dead for decades.

My head was spinning as I stumbled backward, away from the grave markers.

My snowshoes crossed behind me and I fell and landed on a snowbank. Cold seeped through my clothing. The chill went deeper than the dropping temperature and the icy snow beneath me. I felt it in my bones.

I didn't know what was happening. But I did know that if I stayed here any longer, the bitter feeling would never leave. It would take hold of me and drag me down into the frozen ground. Down beneath the headstones. Down to join the others.

I knew I had to fight the urge to surrender. A surge of adrenaline pulsed through my veins, making me feel very much alive. At the same time, my senses were screaming at me to flee. In an instant I bolted to my feet. I pumped my legs as fast as they could go.

Don't look, I told myself as I rushed past the ruins again, not daring to give them a second glance. I knew if I saw a figure in the shadows of the fallen roof, or a face peering out from behind a jagged, broken pane of glass, my heart might stop beating in my chest. I might literally die from fear.

The forest seemed to go on forever as I retraced my path. The elongated, misshapen impressions I'd left with my snowshoes looked more monsterlike than human now. Ignoring the thought, I pressed on with my head down and heart drumming in my ears. Instinct came first. Thinking was secondary. The only way to survive was to move forward.

I was trembling uncontrollably by the time I reached the front porch of the cabin. Stripping the snowshoes, I tossed them aside and burst through the door.

Mom's name was on my lips, but I didn't have to call for her. She was standing right there in the entryway, the last place I'd seen her. But this time, she was wearing her winter coat. Her keys were in hand. She took one look at my face and dropped them. "Oh, honey, what's wrong? Why are you here? You're pale as a ghost."

I buried myself in her arms, relishing the extra softness and warmth of her down-filled sleeves as they encased me. "It was awful," I gurgled. "There's no school. I mean, there is, but it's gone. Instead, there's all these headstones. They're for . . . for the students in my class."

My mother took a step back to look me in the eye. "Sweetheart, you're not making any sense."

"They're all dead!"

Mom stiffened, then let out a heavy sigh. "What are you talking about? You just saw your classmates yesterday."

"On my computer. Not in real life. They aren't real. Mara texted me—"

Mom interrupted me. "See, then. They can't be dead. You must've gotten lost. Around here, that would be enough to scare anyone silly. And you've been pent up for so long. No wonder your imagination ran wild as soon as you reentered the outside world."

I shook my head. "It wasn't my imagination," I said adamantly.

As soon as the words left my mouth, though, I second-guessed myself. Or was it? It all seemed so outlandish from the comfort of my log cabin.

Mom hugged me close again and squeezed. "I'm sorry you got spooked and even sorrier that I have to leave—"

I pulled away. "What? *Now?*"

"I have no choice," Mom said. "It's been a wild morning here, too. There's trouble at Seas the Day. Your dad left fifteen minutes ago to fly back to San Francisco, and we've had some strange readings at the research facility. It's probably nothing, but I have to go check it out. Immediately. It's just a drain so far, but if the entire grid goes down, the consequences could be devastating. And it's my responsibility. I'm sorry," she said again.

Mom sounded uncharacteristically frazzled, which did nothing to soothe my own raging nerves. I knew how much my mom's job meant to her. I couldn't ask her to stay home. So, I asked for the only thing that seemed bearable. "Take me with you?"

Mom scrunched up her face as she considered. "I don't know how long I'll have to be there . . . You'll be bored silly."

"Better than scared to death," I mumbled under my breath, then added, *"Please."* Now that I was home and had put some distance between myself and the graveyard, the utter shock was wearing off. But still, it wouldn't take much to send me over the edge again. A creaky floor, or flickering light, and I'd be cowering in a corner.

"Do you have homework you can bring with you?"

I hesitated. Homework was the last thing on my mind, but it might be a good distraction. Hopefully I'd be able to bury myself in my history assignment and forget all about the terrible morning I'd had. I nodded. Even if I finished the essay early, I'd rather stare at the ceiling of the research facility all day than be left home alone.

My mom sighed in resignation. "Okay. Grab your stuff. Tomorrow, I'll drive you to school and we can get this sorted out."

I wanted to believe that was true. I wanted to think that everything that had happened could be sorted out. I liked order and symmetry. I liked it when things made sense, and I'd never been a fan of the unknown. But something told me that there wasn't an easy explanation for what I'd seen today.

CHAPTER 6

I'd been to the research facility once before. It was a gray, block-shaped building surrounded by overhead wires and a tall, cylindrical turbine. According to Mom, some of the "world's most innovative advances" took place inside. You'd never guess it from its outward appearance.

Mom was in "Dr. Rodriguez mode" and had been lost in thought for the entire drive. Not that I'd felt like talking anyway. The morning's strange turn of events had left me feeling raw. I'd imagined myself finally making new friends today, not being horror-stricken and then hiding from my classmates by shadowing Mom at work.

As we entered the facility, we were greeted by an old man. Despite the number of wrinkles on his face, it seemed as though he neither smiled nor frowned on a regular basis. "Morning, Dr. Rodriguez," he said gruffly, then shot me a sidelong glance.

I squirmed under his observation.

"This is my daughter, Lucy," Mom said. I was thankful when she proceeded to wrap a comforting arm around my shoulder.

It occurred to me that this man was a security guard. Not *a* security guard, *the* security guard. I'd heard Mom mention him before. His name was Harold. His name had come up during a conversation I'd overheard about the "skeleton crew" and how difficult it was to staff the facility in such a remote location.

"Our only line of defense is a man over eighty," were Mom's exact words. "He's White Pine's oldest resident, for heaven's sake."

"It's a good thing you're located in the middle of nowhere, then," Dad replied. "Who would break in? They'd have to find the place first."

Mom had chuckled, but she clearly hadn't found Dad's response all that reassuring.

Now that I'd seen Harold with my own eyes, I wondered if Mom had underestimated the man. He was old. But he had a large frame and there was something intimidating about his stony expression.

Harold grunted while his chin dipped a fraction of an inch as if to say he'd let me through this one time, but only because the head researcher was vouching for me. Apparently, he wasn't convinced I didn't pose a threat.

I was on edge as we skirted past him. Maybe it was his hard stare, or maybe I was bound to feel unsettled for the rest of the day. Probably the latter.

When Mom left me by myself in the break room, the separation made me more anxious than when she'd dropped me off for the first day of summer camp. I knew I couldn't stay glued to her side all day—she had equipment to check and needed to search for the cause of the unusual readings, and I'd only get in the way. But I really didn't want to be left alone, especially in unfamiliar surroundings. I tried to settle in, but the break room was every bit as unwelcoming as the rest of the building—cold, tiled floor; harsh, fluorescent lights; a table; and some chairs. It didn't provide the soothing warmth that I craved, but at least I was far away from the tiny graveyard and, depending on my wavering confidence in the octogenarian security guard, it was a secure location.

As I set to work on my essay about the War of 1812, I realized that Ms. Grant had never once assigned any current-event topics. Did that mean something? I shivered like I'd stepped into a shadow. Because I'd been afraid that Mara or one of the others would try to connect with me online, I left my Chromebook at the cabin. I'd planned on working on my essay the old-fashioned way, with pen and paper, but I was still too rattled to focus.

I chewed on the pencil eraser while my mind wandered back to the tiny graveyard. Were the twelve headstones related to the ruins? They had to be, right? Maybe it was a mistake to leave my laptop behind. As soon as I was reunited with it, I'd have to google the fire. I was so lost in thought that I didn't notice when someone entered the room behind me.

When I heard a loud thunk, followed by a softer thud, I jerked my head up. It was Harold. The noise had been the sound of him setting a stainless-steel water bottle on the table and then dropping a brown paper sack beside it. I watched him warily as he took a seat across from me and then removed a single item from the bag: a can of Vienna sausages.

After popping open the lid, Harold dug his fingers inside the can and retrieved a cold, hot dog–shaped piece of meat. He jammed the entire thing in his mouth. Which was weird enough before you factored in that he did all this without saying a word.

I felt slightly repulsed by his eating habits, not that I let on. Instead, I smiled politely while wondering if I should start a conversation. When the questions I'd planned on asking my classmates flooded my mind—What's your favorite movie? Are there any good hangout spots in White Pine? What kinds of outdoor activities do you all do?—my stomach really started to hurt. Were my classmates actually dead? Had I been talking to ghosts for the past six months? But that wasn't possible. There had to be another explanation. Yet, I'd seen their headstones with my own eyes. So, what then? Was I somehow at the center of an elaborate hoax?

Harold and I sat in awkward silence as my thoughts spiraled, until a young woman entered the break room. "Hey, there!" she said. "I heard we had a visitor."

I was so grateful for the interruption that I actually smiled. A real smile, not the plaster one I'd given Harold. "Yeah, hi. I'm Lucy," I said. Then I shook the woman's outstretched hand. Her chin-length hair was wavy. She wore it pushed back behind her ears, so that her cat eye–shaped glasses stood out even more on her face. Her smile was broad and self-assured, and her lab coat was identical to the one Mom wore, even though this dainty woman had to be decades younger.

"Yes, you are!" The woman said. "I'm Ciara, and you're very welcome here. Young people are a rarity in White Pine. From what I understand, they always have been. Isn't that right, Harold?"

"Uh-huh," Harold mumbled in agreement.

"I hear there was a mishap at your school today. White Pine Secondary, right? Your mom—" Ciara was interrupted by the sound of Harold's water bottle clanking to the table. Our attention was drawn to the noise.

When Ciara saw that Harold had merely knocked it over with his elbow, she started talking again. "Your mom asked if I knew where it'd moved to, but I'm not familiar with it. Are you?" she asked Harold as he righted his bottle.

The security guard shook his head, but there was something unreadable in his eyes. It was almost as though the topic made him uncomfortable. *Or maybe all topics make him uncomfortable*, I thought, considering how little he seemed to talk.

"Anyway, if you want to take a break from your schoolwork, I'd be happy to show you around," Ciara offered, then quickly added, "I don't think your mom will have the time."

It was an easy decision. I packed my stuff up in a heartbeat, then gave Harold a curt wave as I exited the room. I wasn't surprised when he didn't wave back.

There wasn't a lot to see. The building was a mix of offices, labs, and industrial space, and I had to fake interest as Ciara led me around the research facility. To be fair, it might've been more interesting on a day when my world hadn't been turned upside down.

"It's really exciting to be a part of this project," Ciara said while we walked. She pointed out different areas, the computer mainframe, and various pieces of equipment. "Really, what we're doing here could revolutionize how energy is sourced. It's a total fluke how it was discovered, but there's all this untapped potential due to the combination of White Pine's super rare minerals and geothermal activity. If we can just stabilize the fusion of the geothermal energy with the energy stored in the area's mineral deposits, it could turn the world of science on its head."

I tuned out most of what Ciara said, but her "fluke" comment caught my attention. Mom had only mentioned that it was a unique opportunity to work at this research facility. She hadn't explained why we had to move to this ridiculously remote area to do it. "How was it discovered?" I asked.

"Well . . ." Ciara stopped walking and crossed her arms. "So, for years, people have been reporting what they thought was paranormal activity in the surrounding area. Absurd, right?"

My skin crawled and my stomach muscles clenched. "Paranormal activity?"

"Yeah—lights and apparitions—that sort of thing. Some said they heard voices and screams. But a coyote howl can sound an awful lot like a woman shrieking in the night."

I could tell from Ciara's dismissive tone that she didn't believe any of the claims. But alarm bells were screeching in my head. If there was paranormal activity in White Pine, it might explain some of the creepiness I'd been experiencing.

"Eventually a group of scientists from Fairbanks caught wind of it and came to investigate. They discovered a new mineral—one that's phosphorescent, so it gives off this eerie glow in the dark."

I nodded. I'd seen flashes of light in the forest. Ones that shouldn't be there . . .

"That combined with steam from the geothermal hot springs," Ciara continued, "and well, mystery solved. Best part is, harvesting the energy from the phantomium—that's what the researchers named it—phantom-ium." Ciara chuckled, then leaned in conspiratorially and added, "Who says scientists don't have a sense of humor?"

I wanted to laugh off the silly name the way Ciara had, but I couldn't. Just like I wanted to believe a rare mineral was the root cause of all my troubles, but I couldn't believe that, either.

"Anyway, turns out harvesting energy from phantomium is much safer than getting nuclear power from uranium. There's no radioactive waste. And when a tiny amount is combined with the energy from the springs, the output is incredible."

While Ciara talked, I wrung my hands. When she finished speaking, I blurted out, "Could the phantomium or the geothermal hot springs, could they . . . um, make electronics malfunction?" I didn't see how things in the natural world could account for the graveyard, but my electronics had been going haywire, too. There was that creepy photo on my laptop and the woman sobbing. My alarm hadn't gone off after I set it, and my sewing machine had powered on all by itself.

Ciara frowned. "What do you mean?"

"Could they cause something, like a sewing machine or speakers, to turn on suddenly for no reason?"

"I don't know, that doesn't sound like anything I read about in the reports, but . . . sometimes electronics will behave unexpectedly if there is some sort of electrical interference nearby. Bad wiring, power surges, nearby power lines, or other electrical devices can all cause malfunctions. Why? Do you have some faulty electronics that are giving you trouble? You might want to toss them if you do."

I shrugged. "No reason, just curious." Malfunctions or not, I couldn't part with my laptop or phone—I was isolated enough without losing my only connections to the outside world, and my grandmother's sewing machine was irreplaceable.

For the rest of the tour, I pretended to listen and gave a courteous nod whenever Ciara introduced me to one of the other employees, but I couldn't stop thinking about what she said. The reports of paranormal activity sounded different from what I'd experienced, but they had to be related. And how were my classmates involved? As much as I wanted to believe a rare mineral was to blame, it couldn't account for everything I'd been through.

So, what then? Were my classmates truly dead, or had Mara and the others, knowing White Pine was a place where freaky things occurred, been playing on that to fuel my fright? I'd been so sure they were ghosts when I'd been standing in the grave-yard. Now an elaborate prank seemed more likely. Still, I wasn't completely convinced. I needed more information. More than anything, I wanted answers.

CHAPTER 7

It was well past the end of the school day by the time my mom was ready to leave. As she drove us home, she seemed to be on a different planet. I didn't want to interrupt her thoughts, but what Ciara had said was burning in my mind. Finally, I blurted out, "SO, it was paranormal activity that led to the research facility being built in White Pine?"

Mom blinked several times, then cast a tired, fleeting glance my way.

"I know what you're thinking," Mom said. "But what happened to you this morning, the graves, the students . . . I don't know what's going on exactly, but they aren't ghosts. It's so easy for people's imaginations to get the better of them. Especially when one finds themself alone in a forest."

There was a hard edge to her voice as she continued talking. "What happened here was like the northern lights, right? They were regarded as supernatural for centuries before scientists understood the phenomenon was caused by electrically charged particles entering the earth's atmosphere. When things seem unexplainable, it's only because the explanation is yet to be discovered."

I wasn't sure what I'd done to upset her. The harsh tone stung a bit until I realized Mom was talking as much to herself as she was to me. No doubt her level of frustration was related to her work. She hadn't been successful in uncovering the source of the mysterious readings.

I let the topic go, and we fell into silence again. There was no sense in making Mom more irritable by pressing the issue. As for the northern lights, there was a part of me that liked the idea of gods and monsters causing the purple, green, yellow, and red streaks of color across the sky more than I liked knowing the science behind it. I'd always thought of myself as having a logical mind, just like Mom, but now it was one more thing I wasn't sure about.

I stared out the window. There were no colorful streaks in the sky tonight—only white streaks of snow flying toward our windshield. As soon as the wipers swished them away, new ones took their place.

The first thing I did when I got home was plug my sewing machine back in. It didn't start whirring again, but I scanned the air anyway as if I could see the electrical interference Ciara had mentioned. Next, I mustered the courage to flip the on switch and step on the pedal. *Nothing.* Still no *ch ch ch* and the needle didn't move up or down. It acted like it had no power at all. Apparently, the problem was the machine itself, then. Faulty wiring? Maybe. Or it was probably just old and had stopped working. The thought made me sad. I could get a new sewing machine, but this one was the only thing I had that once belonged to Grandma Bell. And I missed her. A lot. Losing it felt a little like losing her all over again.

After a few more tries, I stopped procrastinating and flipped open my Chromebook. Despite my nerves, I googled *White Pine Secondary fire.* Of course, the school had to be named after a type of wood. And with wood commonly being used to fuel fires, about fifty million results popped up. I scrolled and scrolled. I know. I should've tried to narrow the results, but I really was nervous about what I might find. My fear was still too fresh to read about the children who'd lost their lives in the ruins.

I gave up and checked my inbox, thinking there might be an email from Ms. Grant inquiring about my absence. As far as I knew, Mom had never found the time to excuse me from school today.

I thought I might also find emails from my classmates. Something along the lines of *ha-ha, we fooled you again.*

As it turned out, the one new email in my inbox wasn't from Ms. Grant or any of the other students. It came from the generic email address for White Pine Secondary. The subject: School Closure. I hastily clicked open the email and read:

White Pine Secondary School will be closed on Friday, April 11, in anticipation of the severe weather in the forecast. All classes will be moved online. In-person learning to resume on Monday, April 14. Stay warm and stay safe!

Mom had mentioned that another snowstorm was blowing in, right on the heels of the last. Still, I didn't know what to make of the message. I read it several times. On the one hand, it was a relief. Given the chance that my classmates might really be the dead souls of children who had died in a tragic school fire, I was terrified to go anywhere near them. Another day at home felt like a stay of execution. I also didn't know if Mom remembered her promise to drive me to school tomorrow—*Dr. Rodriguez* still had problems to sort out at work. It would be better if she didn't have to deal with this, too.

On the other hand, it was aggravating. All day long I'd waffled back and forth between believing my classmates were ghosts, and my mind telling me it was impossible. I didn't know whether to listen to my mind, or my gut, but I did know that the war between them had to stop, or I'd be driven mad. As scared as I was, I didn't know if I could wait until Monday to get to the bottom of things. My mind flashed to the gull that'd been snared by fishing line and then died in the tree. Like the gull, I feared that the longer I was stuck in this predicament, the less likely my escape would be.

By the time I awoke the following morning, Mom had already left for work. I told myself that she must've received the "School Closure" email, too. I didn't want to think Dr. Rodriguez had completely forgotten something so important to me.

The drumming in my chest as I waited for class to begin was so powerful, it almost hurt. I agonized over what the other students would say. Would they threaten me? Would they be cruel?

I held my breath as boxes and faces began popping up on my screen at precisely 8:00 a.m. The image of me, the one captured by my Chromebook's camera, was also projected on the screen. I hated that I appeared so shell-shocked, but I couldn't help it. As I silently searched my classmates' faces for any clue as to what was happening, it didn't surprise me to find that Mara's expression was unreadable. She always seemed in complete control of her emotions.

I kind of expected some of the other students to crack, though. I peered hard into the camera and scowled, hoping that at least Josephine would react. Mara had once called Josephine a "Goody Two-shoes." If anyone would give themselves away with a guilty expression, it would be her. But I just didn't see it.

I moved my stare to Jamie next. He'd be the last to show remorse, but I thought his ego might be so big that he'd have to confess just to get the credit. No, not so much as a smirk.

I couldn't believe it. They were all acting like it was just another day—like everything was perfectly normal. But none of them was saying anything. Not a word. They just sat there in their old-fashioned clothing surrounded by antiques. Why hadn't I realized before that the sewing machine in Josephine's room was ages older than even my hand-me-down machine?

Finally, I couldn't take it anymore. "What is going on?!" I practically screamed at the screen.

"Why, Lucy, whatever are you talking about?" Mara asked innocently.

"We missed you at school," Jamie added. "Why didn't you join us?"

"Join you?" I wanted to stay calm, but I couldn't. "Join you? There was no school. Just gravestones. With *your* names on them." I sounded hysterical, but I didn't care.

There was silence for a moment, and then . . . laughter. It was eerie, the way it sounded, both echoey and hollow as chuckles and snickers from the twelve others crackled through my Chromebook speakers.

"You're jesting, right?" Mara asked, and the others hushed to hear my response.

"No." I shook my head. "The map, the one you sent, led me straight to a graveyard by the ruins. A graveyard for all of you." I was repeating myself now, but I didn't know what else to say to make them drop this charade.

Mara tilted her head. "Are you feeling unwell? Was it fever that kept you from us? You seem to have experienced some sort of delirium."

My mouth gaped open. It was still open when Ms. Grant's message popped up in the chat box. "Enough chitchat. Back to work."

My bewilderment only grew worse as the day went on. Not only did the others treat me like I'd imagined the whole thing, but they were also overly nice, like they pitied me for my confusion. Even Josephine was condescending. I couldn't imagine ever wanting to be friends with her, with any of them, after this. It was humiliating.

Thank goodness it was Friday. If I couldn't get the truth out of them, at least I'd have a few days' break from White Pine Secondary and its students. I hoped it would be enough time to figure things out, or . . . maybe even transfer to a new school. Once the idea popped into my head, I latched on to it. I'd been embarrassed to let my parents know I was being bullied again.

But this crossed the line. I needed out, and for that to happen, my parents would have to know why.

As soon as Mom got home from work that evening, I burst from my room and met her in the hallway. "Mom, please. I *have* to switch schools. Immediately. Everything is awful. The students are mean. They keep teasing me and I think they're planning something terrible." I bit my tongue before letting it slip again that I thought there was a chance they might also be dead. No doubt, Mom would find the issue of me being bullied a more reasonable argument than if I insisted they were ghosts.

While I waited for her to answer, I took in Mom's appearance. She looked as though she was carrying the weight of the world. Her eyes were tired, and her shoulders were drooping, and I could tell my pleas weren't helping any. But, still, this was important. I was truly terrified of my classmates.

"Take a deep breath," Mom said after letting out her own puff of air.

I did, then said, "I think they might harm me." I hadn't fully realized it until that moment, but prank or no prank, I truly thought Mara and the others were dangerous.

Mom looked me in the eye. "Did they threaten to hurt you?"

"Well, no, not exactly . . ."

"What happened today? What did they say?"

"They laughed when I told them about the graves I found,

and then they were nice. *Too* nice." As soon as the words left my mouth, I knew I'd made a mistake. I'd brought up the graves again, and Mom already didn't believe me about those. She cast me a soft smile, but that was the last thing I wanted. It was too close to how my classmates had talked down to me when I brought up the graveyard to them.

"I think that's just your anxiety talking, don't you?"

I didn't respond.

"Give it more time," Mom said. "You haven't even met the other students in real life yet. Everyone is different online. These freak storms are bound to stop, and once you get past this transition, and you're going to school every day, I know you'll make some friends." On that note, she pecked my forehead with a kiss and walked away.

I plodded back into my room, upset I hadn't been able to get through to Mom. It was dark now even though I knew I'd left the light on. I immediately flipped the switch, and the sudden brightness was blinding. When I recovered, I was relieved to see that everything appeared exactly as before. I warily took a few steps forward. As I did, my sewing machine turned itself on again. I about hit the ceiling. Normally, I liked the sound, but now the noise of the needle stabbing up and down was chilling. I raced across the room to unplug it.

I took a few deep breaths and tried to tell myself that it was all some sort of electrical interference. Ciara did say that was a thing. Maybe what was happening with my stuff was all completely normal and harmless. But that's not what my gut was saying, and I was more afraid than ever. Whether living or dead, my classmates had found a way to terrorize me even after the school day had ended.

CHAPTER 8

I hardly slept that night and was on edge the moment I got up Saturday morning. Would my sewing machine act up again, or another freaky photo appear on my laptop? Everywhere I went inside the cabin, I felt jittery and jumpy, not knowing what to expect next.

In a way, it was like what Dad called cabin fever. Only much worse. Dad suffered from it, too—when he was here, anyway. Thinking of him made me jealous. He was in San Francisco, soaking up sunshine. He was far from the never-ending Alaskan winter, Mom's foul mood, horrible classmates, and the tiny graveyard. How I wished he'd taken me with him.

For half a second, I considered sending Hana a text or an email, to get her take on all this madness. But I didn't think my heart could handle being ignored again. I still didn't understand it. For the first month or so after the move, we texted back and forth like nothing changed. Then one day, Hana stopped texting back. I kept spamming her for weeks, thinking she had too much homework or she'd somehow missed my gazillion messages, but that she'd get around to it eventually. She never did respond, though, and now I only sent an occasional text.

I tried not to think about missing Hana, just like I tried not to think about the headstones engraved with my classmates' names. It was no use. I'd run my fingers through the crevices in the stone. They weren't fakes. It all seemed too elaborate to be a joke. But if it wasn't a joke, what was it? The other students had laughed it off. They'd dismissed my story and tried to make me believe I'd imagined the whole thing. Mara even asked if I'd had a fever.

I ran a high fever once when I had the flu, and honestly, it did cause me to see things that weren't there. Like, I had a poster of a skateboarder riding a half-pipe hanging on my bedroom wall. While I was feverish, I imagined the skateboarder flying off the ramp and into my room. No joke, I was having a conversation about grind and slide tricks with the nonexistent skateboarder when Mom came in to bring me medicine. We laughed about it for days after my fever broke.

What I'd gone through the past few days was different. It didn't have the same feverish dream feel to it. Not to mention

I hadn't run an actual fever for months. Other than cabin fever, but that didn't count. Or did it? Could being stuck indoors too long have the same effect on a person as physical illness? The more time that passed, the more I doubted myself. By midmorning, I couldn't take it any longer.

Mom was working in her home office again. I lightly tapped on the door, then poked my head in through the open crack. "Okay if I go out and do a little snowshoeing?"

There were sheets and sheets of data spread across Mom's desk. She kept her eyes on her work. "Uh-huh," she said.

"If I'm not back in a few hours, you might want to check the graveyard in case my classmates truly are ghostly spirits intent on my demise."

"Sounds good, honey."

I sighed. It would be nice if both my parents weren't MIA as I tried to figure out what on earth was going on.

The storm had passed, and sunlight glistened off the snow. It was a beautiful day. I still shivered as soon as I took one step outside. This was it. I was going to track down my answers. It would be exhilarating if I wasn't so scared.

My usual path was slushy again today. As I slogged through the snow, I started to question myself. Was I being stupid? There was a good chance I was playing right into my classmates' hands. But I had to know. I had to see for myself whether I'd imagined the graveyard and the headstones or if they were real. Even though I never wanted to see any of it again, I had to.

A cool breeze picked up. The whistling wind was unnerving as it rustled through branches and pine needles. By then, my cabin was out of view, and I had the same sensation as I'd had before—that there was someone in the trees, watching my every move.

"Who's there?" I cried out.

There was no response at first, but then . . . laughter. At least, I thought it was laughter. The noise was soft and crackling. It could've been a combination of the wind and my mind playing tricks on me again, or . . . it could have been the sound of someone trying to stifle their amusement.

I sped up. The sooner I got to the tiny graveyard, the sooner I could return home. As I went, I shivered again. What if I was walking straight into a trap? Had my classmates known that if they pretended like nothing had happened, then I'd have to come back to investigate? They'd asked me so many questions but hardly answered any of mine. They knew me way better than I knew them. They'd know I'd be curious. That I wouldn't cower at home forever.

Lost in thought, I didn't see the branch, or the boy, until it was too late. I heard a snap. My mind registered movement but not where it was coming from. Out of fear, I froze. The next thing I knew, arms were wrapping around my stomach, stealing the air from my lungs as I was knocked off my feet.

Our arms, legs, and my snowshoes tangled together as we flew. We landed, still knotted together, on a snowbank a few feet away. A split second later, a massive branch landed right where I'd last been standing. The limb had plummeted from high in the tree above. If the boy hadn't tackled me to the ground, I would've been crushed. But because I was already feeling paranoid, my first instinct was to fight off my attacker.

I wriggled free and sprang to my feet, holding my fists up, ready to swing. I really thought it was Jamie or maybe Peter or Henry. But when I got a good look, I could see that this boy was smaller than any of the boys in my class. His face was unfamiliar. His expression said he was afraid, not out to hurt someone. Then there was the fact that the tree branch could've killed me if he hadn't carried me out of harm's way.

Not attacker. Rescuer.

The anger that had flared inside me burnt out quickly, leaving shock in its place. I dropped my fists and clutched my stomach. I shook slightly as I spat out, "Who . . . who are you?"

The boy dropped his gaze. He hesitated before answering. When he spoke, his voice sounded crackly and weak. It was barely above a whisper as he said, "Connor. My name is Connor."

He looked to be about my age. He had red hair, his brown

eyes were flecked with green, and his cheeks were hollow. He seemed to swim inside his gray wool coat and beanie. His leather boots looked warm, but he didn't have snowshoes. "Thank you, Connor," I said. "I'm Lucy." After a moment of awkward silence, I added, "Where did you come from?"

Connor clambered to his feet. When he spoke this time, his voice was steadier. "I live not too far from here, at the homestead near Blue River Gulch."

I didn't know of any homesteads in the area. But I'd been stuck indoors practically the entire time I'd lived here; I wasn't aware of anything in the area other than the school and the research facility.

"Why don't you go to White Pine Secondary?" I asked.

The boy's eyes widened. "My parents don't want me anywhere near there. I'm homeschooled."

"Do you know the students?" I pressed.

Connor seemed uneasy as he sidestepped my question. "You should stay away, too," he said. "There's something not right about them and that school."

My heart skipped a beat. He wasn't wrong . . . "What do you know?" I took a step forward while searching his face for clues.

He backed away like a frightened animal. "Don't go!" I called. "Please?"

Connor stopped in his tracks, and I continued.

"I'm new here," I said. "I don't know *anyone*. I haven't seen *anything*. Do you think, I mean, could you maybe . . . show me around? There must be something around here other than just trees?" Alarm bells quietly sounded in my head. *You don't know this boy*, I thought. *Can you trust him?* But that was silly. I couldn't be paranoid for the rest of my life just because of what my classmates were putting me through. He'd saved me from the falling branch. If I couldn't trust him, who could I trust?

Connor shuffled his feet in the snow. He didn't meet my eyes and his hesitance made me wonder if he'd been bullied, too. He said he was homeschooled now, but maybe my classmates had played the same trick on him before I came along.

When he finally stopped fidgeting, he asked, "What would you like to see?"

My mind immediately went to the tiny graveyard. But I thought bringing it up now might ruin my chances for any sort of friendship. I'd been cut off from the real world for months, but I still knew it would be weird to ask him if he wanted to go check out some headstones with me after we literally just met. So, I shrugged. "What *should* I see?"

Connor's face lit up. "The river," he said, then shyly added, "it's my favorite place in all of White Pine."

I couldn't help but smile. It was cute the way he'd gotten so excited about a river. Not cute in a "make me weak in the knees" sort of way. But cute in a sweet way. Something about Connor seemed more innocent than all the boys I'd known in San Francisco.

I cast a quick glance in the direction of the graveyard. It was hard to walk away when I'd come this far. My answers might be right around the corner. But I couldn't pass up the opportunity to make a new friend. Now, more than ever, I wanted to connect with someone my own age—someone in White Pine who didn't terrify me.

CHAPTER 9

The river really was wonderful. It was powerful and peaceful all at once. Connor led me to a spot that was postcard pretty. It had billowy, white snowbanks, towering pine trees, giant boulders, swirling pools, and cascading crystal-blue water.

A dreamy expression blossomed on his face. "Do you like to fish?" he asked.

"I . . . I don't know. I've never gone fishing before."

"Are you kidding? It's my favorite thing to do."

"Why?" I genuinely wanted to know. Fish were cold and slimy and the way I saw it, they belonged where they were found—in water. Not above it.

"Well, first they're delicious."

"Eh . . ."

"And second, I like the way when a fish bites the hook, it's almost always unexpected. Everything can seem dull, and it feels like nothing will ever change, but then, one little nibble and your whole day turns around. You have to try it!"

I wasn't entirely convinced, but I liked his enthusiasm. Plus, it was impossible to say no to a smile that big.

Connor showed me how to make a fishing rod from a stick and some line and a hook he carried in his jacket pocket. Then he fashioned one for himself and walked me through the steps of casting. I tried to concentrate on learning how to fish, but from the moment he first pulled out the line, it reminded me of the dead gull.

"What's wrong?" Connor asked. "You look pale."

I shook my head. "It's nothing."

The way he looked into my eyes made me think he could see all the way to my soul. Hana was like that, too. She always knew when I was upset but was pretending I wasn't. I tried to keep my Bailey Henderson problems a secret from her, but she could tell. And she tried to make things better for me, by bringing me shaved ice when I had a rough day, or even just hanging out so we could talk. She had no trouble making new friends in middle school, but she never made me feel any less important to her. That was until after I moved to Alaska.

Connor watched me with a concerned look, then he suddenly brightened. "I know. I'll bring you back in a few weeks so you can see the salmon run," he said. "You won't believe your eyes.

The fish swim up the falls. Oh, and the bears! They snag the salmon out of the air."

That he was already inviting me to do something made me happy. More than that, I could tell he'd been trying to cheer me up. He seemed to actually care about my feelings. Mara and the others had put on a good show in the beginning, before they revealed their terrifying true selves. But now that I thought about it, whenever they talked about meeting me, the conversation had always centered around *their* excitement. Not once had they asked me how I was feeling—if I was nervous or even adjusting okay to living in Alaska. They'd grilled me for information about California, but it seemed like it had been for their own interest, not because they cared what my life there had really been like.

I'd known Connor for less than an hour and already he'd shown me more true kindness than any of my new classmates had. I could almost fool myself into thinking that this was a normal budding friendship on a normal weekend day.

Since Connor was on the quiet side, I asked questions while we were fishing to try to draw him out. I learned that he had one brother, and even though the growing season was short, his family grew potatoes, turnips, and barley on their homestead.

"What about *your* family?" he asked shyly.

"My mom's a scientist. My dad owns a surf shop," I said.

Connor bobbed his head politely, "That's great," he said, but he didn't ask a ton of follow-up questions the way my classmates had.

Even so, it felt right—a real conversation instead of an interrogation. "What else do you like to do?" I asked. "Other than fishing, I mean."

He took his time answering. "I like climbing trees," he said at last. "I really like trees."

"Okay. So, tell me what you like about them."

"The variety. They're all so different." Then he proceeded to name the surrounding trees for me: "Sitka spruce, western hemlock, tamarack, white spruce, and western red cedar." When he was finished, he cast me a lopsided grin and said, "Your turn."

"I used to skateboard a lot when I lived in California," I said. "Oh, and I like to sew. If you want, I can sew you a pouch, so you don't have to carry your hooks and line in your coat pocket."

His face lit so bright, you'd think I'd offered him the moon.

I dropped my stick and let the line go slack. The fish weren't biting, but he seemed happy just the same. While he continued casting, I sat on a rock by the bank and let the icy river water run through my fingertips until they turned purple and numb. I lifted my face toward the sun and welcomed the warmth on my skin. It felt great, but before long, my mind wandered back to my troubles, and I couldn't help but try to find out what Connor knew about White Pine Secondary.

"About the school . . . what happened there?"

Connor stopped casting and went very still. "Nothing good," he mumbled.

"Why don't your parents want you to go near it?"

"It's dangerous," he said. "The original school burnt down a hundred years ago. Thirteen students died. The ruins aren't safe. *Nothing* about that place is safe. That's all I know."

So, it was true. The dates on the headstones read 1925. The school building I'd seen was blackened and charred. It only made sense that the two were connected. "Does everyone around here, um, know about the old school and the fire?" I asked.

While the words were still leaving my mouth, Connor's line grew tight. Thinking it might be a fish, I leaned forward to get a better look.

"Just a snag," Connor said. He focused on freeing the hook and my question went unanswered. All the same, I was starting to form a new theory. I suspected that Mara and Jamie and Josephine weren't really Mara and Jamie and Josephine at all. They were only pretending. Each student in my class must've assumed the name of a child who had died in the fire. A new student—me—had given them an opportunity to pull a prank that went on for months. They weren't excited about me joining their class. Not really. They were excited because their hoax was fun for them. They got a kick out of scaring me and entertainment was hard to come by around here.

All this time the students had pretended their names matched those carved on the headstones, knowing that eventually I'd find the tiny graveyard and be scared out of my mind. It was such a mean thing to do. Thinking about it filled me with rage. What sort of people did something like that? I had a sudden urge to confront my classmates. Any of them. If I could just find out where they lived, I'd knock on their doors. Then they'd have to tell me their real names.

I sprang to my feet. "You asked earlier what I wanted to see. I want to see homes. I want to see the places where the people of White Pine live. There must be some sort of town or neighborhood you can bring me to."

Ciara said she commuted all the way from Fairbanks when she wasn't working remotely. So did most of her coworkers. But my classmates wouldn't drive in from Fairbanks or they'd just go to one of the schools in the city. So, they had to live somewhere close by.

I tried to remember if I'd passed any buildings or structures when I'd gone to work with Mom. I'd been distracted, but I couldn't remember any. And when we first arrived here, we'd flown in on a puddle jumper and driven directly to the cabin. We had our food delivered weekly and hadn't been to a single restaurant or supermarket. Still, there had to be some sort of civilization to see other than the school ruins, my family's cabin, and the research facility.

Connor stood up, too. Then he looked down at his feet while saying, "I can't take you that far."

I'd forgotten he wasn't wearing snowshoes. *Darn*. I let my gaze travel above the tree line. That's when I noticed a wisp of smoke rising in the air. I nodded toward it. "What about there?" I asked. Where there was smoke, there were humans. If I looked for the source, I thought I'd at least find a campfire; at best, the home of one of my classmates.

Connor's attention darted to the smoke, then quickly returned to his feet.

I was confused. "Don't you want to come?"

Connor said nothing.

It wasn't a "yes," but it wasn't a "no," either. "Well, let's go, then," I said, and started walking. I was glad when he followed. He walked behind me, stepping on my tracks where the snow was mostly packed down for him. But even though he chose his steps carefully, his boots broke through the thin crust, and he sunk in the wet, heavy snow.

I plowed ahead just the same. I didn't mean to be inconsiderate, but we were on the move now and I was focused on reaching my destination. Plus, I'd already been gone for hours. Eventually, Mom would come out of her work fog and wonder where I'd gone.

The thing was, I didn't slow down at all to let Connor catch up. I figured it would be impossible to lose the path I was laying out for him, and I told myself I'd stop and wait whenever I got to where the smoke was coming from. Was it where one of my classmates lived? I couldn't wait to find out.

But what would I say? Could I actually confront the student and demand a real name? I was in my own world thinking about it. My chest grew tight as I plodded forward, rounded a bend, and then there it was. A tiny cabin sat right in front of me. It was old and rustic and if it wasn't for the wisps of smoke escaping the chimney, well, I would've thought it was abandoned.

I blew out a breath, then finally peered back, expecting to see Connor still straggling behind. My view went as far as the bend. Up until that point, there was one set of tracks in the snow, and no Connor. I waited, thinking he'd step out from the clump of trees at any moment. I waited. And waited. Still no Connor.

"Connor!" I called out his name. When he didn't respond, I called out a second time, and then a third.

The front door of the tiny cabin swung open behind me. "What's all the racket?"

The old man's gruff voice gave me a scare. I jolted again when I swung around to find Harold facing me. I'd hoped to find a familiar face, but not one belonging to the security guard.

"Lucy?" he said. "Why are you here?"

I forced a smile and offered up a shrug. "I'm exploring White Pine," I said. "I was hoping to find some more people my age."

He humphed. "I thought Ciara made it clear that it's a lost cause."

"Nothing is clear," I grumbled, mostly to myself.

"Does your mother know you're here?"

"Nah, she's too distracted with work stuff." I could hear the hurt in my voice. I hoped Harold couldn't.

He scanned the area surrounding his cabin. So, I scanned it, too, wondering what he expected to see. He wouldn't know to look for Connor, would he?

Finally, he said, "Well, I'm not going to stand here with the door open all day. You can come on in if you'd like."

I really wished Connor would appear. But I knew he'd had plenty of time to catch up if he was still coming.

Did he ghost me, then? I felt a swell of regret. I probably deserved it the way I'd pushed him to come and then rushed ahead like he wasn't even there. The thing was, I really liked him, and I hated to think I'd just spoiled my one chance at having an actual friend.

My eyes did a final sweep of the trees. Then, against my better judgment, I nodded before removing my snowshoes and stepping inside Harold's cabin.

CHAPTER 10

Not only was Harold's home dimly lit, but a thick, musky smell hung in the air. I couldn't blame him for the dust, really. He apparently lived alone, worked full-time and, I mean, he was old. Things built up. Particles of dirt and dead skin cells gathered in cracks and crevices and remained there no matter how hard someone tried to freshen things up. I just hoped I didn't seem too grossed out as I lingered barely six inches inside the door.

Harold looked me up and down, and his gaze felt sharp. "Why are you here?" He asked a second time.

I guess he hadn't accepted my first answer—that I'd been out exploring and looking for people my own age. It wasn't a lie, but it wasn't the complete truth, either. The real reason was: I wanted answers. I could've left as soon as I found out none of my classmates lived here. It's not like Harold was the type to mind if people didn't hang around to visit. But when Ciara had mentioned White Pine Secondary in front of him, I'd gotten the impression that Harold knew more than he was letting on. He'd even knocked over his water bottle when it came up, and not because he was clumsy.

So, I got right to the point. "What do you know about White Pine Secondary School?"

Harold didn't so much as flinch this time. His answer came after a long, deliberate pause. "Until yesterday, I hadn't heard that name used in decades." Another pause. "Why don't you come sit down."

I followed him down the narrow hallway. As I did, I noticed a door cracked open on the right. Harold hastily pulled it closed, but not before I saw an old rocking horse and a train set on the floor. They were both caked with dust. Clearly, they hadn't been played with in ages, but who did the toys belong to? Harold had agreed that children were a rarity in White Pine.

With each step I took, my unease grew. There was nothing welcoming about Harold's home. It felt like a place where things went forgotten and got left behind. When he led me into a cramped den, I saw the source of the rising smoke—a wood-burning stove in the corner. Fire danced and licked at the glass front. The stove had the opposite effect of making me feel warm. It reminded me of the school fire and how Connor said thirteen children died, and looking at the flames made my skin prickle.

I moved my attention to the one small window on the far wall and took in the open field and the scattered trees behind the glass. Connor's hair would stick out like a sore thumb in the snowy scenery. I hoped to see a spot of red dotting the landscape.

"What are you looking for?" Harold asked. "Who's out there?"

"It's nothing," I said, turning from the window. "Just a boy I met. I think he might've left."

Something about my answer seemed to displease him, but it was hard to tell. Everything seemed to displease him. When he lowered himself into a recliner, I took a seat on an oak chair with a thin, well-worn cushion and waited for him to speak.

"My grandparents were immigrants," he started. "They came to Alaska in search of land and citizenship. It was a tough life. Their journey overseas was difficult enough. Then there was a train ride across the country, after which they began the most difficult leg of the journey—the trip north from Oregon. Two of their four children didn't survive the expedition. My father was the youngest. He was a baby when his family claimed their stake. His brother, and only living sibling, was twelve. My grandparents could've used their oldest on the farm, or sent him to the mines, but instead they sent him to school at White Pine Secondary. When my father was old enough, he would've gone as well. The school burned down before he had a chance."

The way Harold waited for my reaction, I could tell he was trying to gauge if this last bit of information came as a surprise. It didn't. I nodded and he went on. "They made the difficult trek to Alaska because they wanted a better life for their children. Between the fever on the trail and the fire once they got here, my father was the only one of his siblings to survive." Harold let out a heavy sigh. "Only a handful of families had settled in White Pine to begin with. Almost an entire generation was lost when the school went up in flames."

The wood-burning stove created an eerie glow, casting shadows across the old man's face. I couldn't imagine what those families, including Harold's, had gone through. It was a long time ago, but still, it seemed wrong and disrespectful for my classmates to turn it into a joke.

"Do you know what caused the fire?" I asked.

"It's a bit of a mystery. My father said the roof collapsed before any of the students could escape. The teacher was dragged from the building, but with all the soot coating her lungs, she died before she could tell her rescuers what happened. Thirteen children were lost that day. It's odd, though, once the fire was extinguished, the remains of only twelve children were recovered. Because of the burns, they were"— Harold cleared his throat—"unrecognizable. No one knows the identity of, or what happened to the thirteenth child. My dad always thought the one whose remains weren't found must've been the one who started the fire."

A shiver ran up my spine. Why hadn't it occurred to me when Connor mentioned that thirteen children had died in the fire that the total didn't match the number of headstones I'd counted at the graveyard? Had there ever been thirteen graves? The names on the headstones were the same names my twelve class-mates had given me. Who had been left out? Who was the thirteenth child? Was the missing grave the key to it all?

"I didn't know the school had been reopened," Harold com-mented. "Change comes slower here, but it does come eventually."

That he was so calm unnerved me more. But something about what he'd said reminded me of my conversation with Ciara. The research facility would've been a huge change for White Pine. "The phantomium," I blurted out.

"What about it?"

"Did your dad mention ever seeing lights or hearing noises in the forest when he was a kid? Have *you* seen anything strange?"

Harold bristled, then abruptly stood up and said, "Tell your mother I said hello."

That was my cue to go. It was probably for the best. I'd been here too long already and the longer I stuck around, the more uncomfortable I felt. Still, as I rose to my feet, I wished I knew how to read the old man. It could be that I'd just outworn my welcome. But if he'd given me the brush-off to avoid talking about the phantomium, did that mean he thought there was more to the sightings than what science could explain?

Either way, I thanked Harold and left. Once outdoors, I gulped in the fresh, frigid air. It wasn't just the dank smell of Harold's cabin that had made me uneasy; there was a darkness about his home, about the man himself. It seemed like his property was the closest one to my family's home, but I didn't foresee any neighborhood barbecues in our future. I never wanted to visit his cabin again.

While I strapped my snowshoes back on, I scanned the area for Connor again. It bothered me that I didn't get a chance to smooth things over or say goodbye. But I wouldn't know where to begin looking for him. He'd walked in my tracks and hadn't left any of his own for me to follow. He said he lived "near Blue River Gulch," but the Blue River stretched on for miles. My heart sank thinking I might never see him again. He'd saved me from that falling tree limb . . . had I made it clear how thankful I was? Did he know I wanted to be friends?

I called Connor's name one last time. The wind had picked up while I was in Harold's cabin. It muffled my voice. That, and the fact that the sun was dipping in the sky, made it seem pointless to keep trying. The chill bit through my clothing as I gave up on finding the boy and started for home.

CHAPTER 11

I was surprised and more than a little relieved to find Mom wasn't worried when I got back. In fact, she seemed in a better mood than when I'd left. Judging by the smile on her face, I thought whatever had been the issue with the research facility, she'd figured it out. She met me in the entryway and pulled me into a hug. "How about some hot cocoa and a midafternoon movie?"

"Really?"

"You bet!"

For a split second, I thought about bringing her up to speed on everything—the tree limb, Connor, my creepy encounter with Harold, my new theory about the prank my classmates were playing on me. Maybe I'd even ask her to reconsider letting me switch schools. But . . . I just couldn't do it. She was the happiest I'd seen her all week, and I didn't want to ruin her good mood. I promised myself I'd tell her everything eventually. We had most of the weekend ahead of us still . . . or so I thought.

Mom bopped around, popping popcorn and preparing our drinks. Extra chocolate powder and marshmallows in mine— just the way I liked it. Then we settled in on the couch in front of the TV with our purple ceramic mugs—ones the size of soup bowls. The marshmallows quickly melted into the hot, sugary, brown liquid. My parents and I had had many movie dates since moving to White Pine. They'd been bright spots during the long, dark winter months. Normally, I'd sit in the middle seat, squished between Mom and Dad. Today, Mom and I snuggled together and draped a fuzzy, warm blanket across our laps.

Mom talked me into an old, animated movie called *WALL·E*. The little Waste Allocation Load Lifter was super cute, but his loneliness at being the last robot left on Earth hit me hard. My thoughts wandered back to Connor. Alaska was a big place, but our paths had crossed once. It could happen again, couldn't it? I sure hoped so. My parents were great, but I desperately wanted a friend. And after the past few days, I knew I'd never be able to trust any of the students from White Pine Secondary.

WALL·E had just met EVE, a sleeker, newer robot sent to Earth on a probing mission, when two things happened at once. The TV made a pop and then displayed nothing but gray static, and an alarm when off in Mom's office. "What now?" Mom grumbled as she hopped up, then went to check on the alarm.

I groaned. "Not again." I punched a few buttons on the remote, trying to get the picture back. It couldn't be just a coincidence that another one of our electronics was having issues, could it? Where was the electrical interference coming from? And how widespread was it? At first, I thought it was just the electronics in my room. Now I wondered if whatever had caused my phone alarm, my screen saver and speakers, my sewing machine, and the TV (the list kept growing!) to go haywire was also behind the problems at the research facility. I clicked off the staticky TV and went to find Mom. Dr. Rodriquez was in her office with her elbows resting on her desk and her fingers pressed to her temples. She glanced up at me. "I don't understand it," she said. "I'd decided that the first readings were just a glitch. But it happened again. I'm so sorry. We'll have to finish *WALL·E* another time. I need to go to the facility to check this out."

"On the weekend?" I didn't mean for my voice to sound whiny, but it did.

Mom sighed. "I'm so sorry, Luce. It can't wait until Monday, and it would take too long for any of the other researchers to make the trip. That was part of the deal when I was offered this job, that I would be on call for emergencies."

But the timing of this emergency was terrible. I thought I'd be able to talk to Mom after the movie. We had a lot to discuss.

One thing in particular seemed important enough to bring up now, even if she was back in crisis mode. "Do you think whatever is happening at the research facility is connected to what just happened with the TV?"

Mom tilted her head. "No, honey, I don't." Her response came quickly, like she hadn't given it any thought. That wasn't like her.

"Can I come with you?" I asked. Maybe we could talk during the car ride. Maybe we could help each other sort things out.

"Not this time," Mom said.

I wanted to protest, but I'd literally wandered around the Alaskan wilderness by myself just hours before. It would be hard to argue that I wasn't old enough to stay home alone. "Okay, no big deal," I said.

But it was a big deal. I'd tried to stay hopeful. All winter long, I'd dreamed of spring and budding friendships, but now . . . everything was such a mess. And, when I needed my parents the most, they were occupied with their own troubles.

I saw Mom to the door and locked it behind her when she left. Then I went straight to my room. It would've been nice to think about something totally unrelated to White Pine Secondary. I would've tried drowning out my thoughts with some sewing tutorials on YouTube, but I didn't want anything to do with electronics at the moment. So, instead I tortured myself by replaying the day's events over and over in my head.

I couldn't stop thinking about what both Harold and Connor had said regarding the thirteen students. Counting on my fingers, I listed the names of my twelve classmates: "Mara, Jamie, Josephine, Henry, George, Elizabeth, Lillian, Walter, Annabel, Ruth, Peter, and Marie." Were they *all* conspiring against me, or were they just going along with whatever Mara told them to do?

I had to get to the bottom of things. I wondered if there was record of the thirteenth student, a class list or something. Would it be sitting in an archive somewhere? Or maybe there was evidence I'd missed back at the tiny graveyard.

My phone startled me when it rang. But I recovered quickly when I saw it was Dad wanting to FaceTime. I joined his call immediately.

"How are things in 'The Last Frontier'?" he asked as soon as his face appeared on my phone screen. "The Last Frontier," I'd learned, was a nickname for Alaska because portions of the largest state had yet to be explored.

I scrunched up my face.

"That good, huh?" The concern in Dad's voice was obvious. "What's up?"

I swallowed a hard lump before talking. "I think . . . I think all the other students here are plotting against me." The corners of my eyes stung as I spoke. "They keep playing mean tricks. And I want to switch schools, but Mom says I should give it more time."

"Oh, kiddo, I'm so sorry," Dad said. "Your mom is right, though. They just don't know how radically cool you are, but they will once they get to know you. Just hang in there, okay?"

That wasn't what I wanted to hear. Not sure I could talk any more about it right now without bursting into tears, I changed topics. "Thanks, Dad. How are things there?"

"Oh, you know, I lost all pigment these past six months. Got a little sun on my pasty skin today and I'm burnt to a crisp. Some computer malfunction caused our internal server to go berserk, and my financial records went up in smoke. Not to mention, I'm thousands of miles away from my girls and I miss you both like mad." Even though his tone was heavy, he said all this with a warm smile on his face. How many times had I heard Mom say his smile was "the perfect antidote for a long day in a cold, sterile lab"?

I'm not saying it was enough to totally turn things around for me, but his lightheartedness did do my soul some good. I cast an almost-smile back at him.

"Forget my woes, I want to know more about your troubles," Dad said. "I heard you still haven't had any I.R.L. classes."

"That's true."

"And these classmates of yours—they are bullying you?"

"That is also true. Well, more like they're trying to scare me to death," I said.

"You know what you need to do, right?"

I sighed loud enough for him to hear. "Ignore them," I said. It was what I'd done with Bailey Henderson after the hair incident.

"Ignoring them will work some, but eventually you'll have to tell them to stop," Dad said.

If only it were that easy.

"I hate that you're going through this, kiddo. If you'd like, I can reach out to your teacher for you."

I shook my head. I didn't bother to tell him that I thought there was something off about Ms. Grant as well. It was strange enough that I'd never seen her face, but she had to be at least somewhat aware of what had been going on. She'd been listening when I'd confronted my classmates about the headstones, but she hadn't stepped in. Why was that?

Because adults were supposed to know better. This would get blown into an even bigger deal if my parents knew Ms. Grant was aware of the bullying and had done nothing. And I didn't want to go through all that on top of everything else. I wanted to lie low until I could convince my parents to let me transfer schools. Maybe I could be homeschooled like Connor. Then I'd never have to deal with any of the White Pine Secondary students or Ms. Grant again.

"Okay," Dad said, "but you can't hide from it. The problem won't go away on its own. You march into school on Monday with your chin up, and you show them what you're made of: smarts and good humor and kindness. Show them that they're a bunch of fools for teasing you, and that they'd all be lucky to have you for a friend."

His words of encouragement turned my almost-smile into a full one. "Yeah," I said.

We spent the next ten minutes talking about the surf (rough), the first stop Dad made once he arrived in San Fran (to pick up a shaved-ice cone), and about Hana Lee and her family, who owned the gift shop next door to Seas the Day. Dad didn't know about the falling out with my best friend. (One more thing I'd decided to keep from my parents.) So, it hurt extra when he reported how well Hana was doing and how happy the Lees all seemed.

When the doorbell rang shortly after Dad and I hung up, I assumed Mom had forgotten her keys or something. I raced to open the door, but it wasn't her who I found standing on the other side. It was Connor.

CHAPTER 12

Seeing him again was like blue skies after a storm. "How did you find me?" I asked with a great big smile on my face.

"Easy." Connor grinned sheepishly. "I went back to where the tree branch fell and followed your tracks. They led me here."

"Ah, nice. Do you want to come in?"

To my delight Connor nodded, then removed his wool cap as soon as he was inside. His red hair was slightly matted to his head, and he nervously ran his fingers through it. For a moment, neither of us said anything. Then, at the exact same time, we both blurted, "I'm sorry."

We both chuckled, then I said, "I didn't mean to leave you behind."

"I'm sorry I disappeared like that," he said.

"Where did you go?"

"Back to the river," he said.

"Right." *I should've known.*

"Were you serious?" he asked.

I had no idea what he was talking about. "Serious about what?"

He twisted his hands around his cap. "That you could sew me a pouch for my fishing gear."

"Absolutely! Do you . . . do you want to pick out the material?"

His hazel eyes brightened when he met my gaze, and he nodded eagerly.

"Okay, then!" As I led him down the hallway to the storage closet, I tried to stay calm. I didn't want to act "too extra," as Bailey Henderson would say when I wore dresses she thought were too colorful, or when I was nervous and laughed too loudly. I didn't want my excitement to scare him off again.

I pulled out every single bolt of fabric I owned. Flowers, paisleys, solids, stripes, polka dots, zigzags, and more. "There's so many," he said.

"Right?" It was why I loved sewing—all the patterns and colors, so many possibilities!

"Will you help me decide?" Connor asked.

"Well, you'll want something durable," I said thoughtfully. "Something fishing hooks won't easily poke through."

He nodded.

I dug through the stack knowing exactly what I was looking for. "What about this one?" I held up a piece of waterproof canvas with a neon camo print.

His grin rose on one side of his face. "It's perfect."

It really was. If it got wet while he was fishing, it wouldn't matter, and the fabric was a heavy enough weight, it could take a beating. To punch through it, I would need to use an extra strong needle on my sewing machine. I—my thoughts stopped cold. I couldn't use my sewing machine. Not when my classmates had found a way to make it stop working. The stab of unrest I felt must've shown on my face because Connor said, "What's wrong?"

"Nothing," I said, flashing him a ghost of a smile. "Do you want a snack?"

Connor shrugged. I took that as a "yes." I refolded the fabric, set it on top of the stack, then started for the kitchen. The thing was, I couldn't shake the heaviness that returned the moment I thought about my sewing machine. Since Connor had turned up, I'd been imagining a future for myself in White Pine. A future with a friend. Someone to hang out with and go do things together. I could picture myself giving him the fishing pouch I would make for him, and then going along the first time he used it.

But—and it was a big "but"—none of that could happen until

I got past this terrible thing that was happening to me. My life was bound to be tough until I could find a way to make Mara and the other students leave me alone.

Once we were in the kitchen, I dumped some cheese crackers in a bowl and set them on the table. Connor took a seat, but I remained standing. "The old man I visited after you left, he said that they only found the remains of twelve children after the fire. You said thirteen died." Connor's face darkened, but I didn't back off. "Do you know anything about what happened to the thirteenth child?"

He smiled weakly. "Why would I?"

"Stay here," I commanded. Then I dashed to my room and returned with my laptop. I sat at the table across from him and flipped it open. I hadn't gotten very far the other night when I'd googled *White Pine Secondary fire*. A bunch of sites on fire bans and wildland fires had popped up, but nothing useful. But I didn't have Connor by my side then. This time I felt braver, and even more motivated. I added *1925* to the end and a bunch of randomness on a century of logging and pine forests filled the first page of results.

"What are you doing?" Connor asked.

"Research," I said.

"I don't think you should. I think you should just forget all about the school. Please."

I studied his face. I couldn't tell if his expression was clouded by fear or something else. But if I was going to face the other students on Monday, I couldn't go in blind, or they'd keep up the charade. I had to call their bluff, and for that, I needed all the information I could find.

"I have to go back," I said with a groan. "My parents are making me." I didn't tell him that I also couldn't sew his fishing pouch until I figured out what was happening with my electronics, and I was pretty sure it was all connected.

"It isn't safe," Connor said.

This time, it was me who shrugged without saying anything. I skimmed the first page of results then clicked to read the next page. I scrolled all the way to the bottom, where something caught my eye.

Worst School Fires in US History. And in the description: *White Pine, Alaska.*

"Don't," Connor pleaded.

He didn't know how important this was. I clicked on the link. I scanned the page, which was just a compilation of the names of schools, the dates of the fires, and the number of lives lost. One in Collinwood, Ohio, where 172 students lost their lives on March 4, 1908. Another in Chicago, where ninety-two students and three nuns died on December 1, 1958.

Then, near the bottom: *White Pine, Alaska. April 13, 1925:*

Twelve students perished when a chimney fire quickly spread and engulfed the one-room classroom.

Narrowing my eyes, I kept scrolling until a black-and-white photo appeared. When I realized what it was, my heart skipped a beat. I couldn't breathe. Right there in front of me, in the century-old photo, were the faces of my twelve classmates. They were standing on the same porch as the one in the creepy photo of the children wearing Halloween costumes. Only in this photo, they weren't wearing masks. Mara, Jamie, and the rest—they'd never pretended to be the children who died. They *were* the children who died.

No, no, no, no, no, no . . . This couldn't be. But it was. It was real. All of it. And . . . my eyes shot to the boy sitting across from me. He was one of them. The thirteenth child. The black-and-white photo didn't do justice to his vibrant red hair, but the sunken cheeks and slight frame gave him away.

"Connor," I choked out his name. He met my eyes with a hollow gaze at the same time the lights flickered out. The cabin was equipped with heavy, room-darkening shades because of the extra summer daylight hours. Even the screen on my laptop went dark, leaving me in pitch blackness. A scream lodged itself in my throat as I punched keys on my laptop. Nothing. I fumbled in the dark for my phone. When my fingers ran across its rubbery case, I snatched it off the table, intending to use it as

96

a flashlight. I pressed every last button, but it wouldn't turn on.

I was too terrified to walk across the room to draw back the drapes. Connor had gone perfectly silent and still the moment the lights went out. "Why are you in the picture?" I demanded. "Tell me."

He didn't answer.

While I sat there in the dark, not knowing what to do, I listened to the sound of my ragged breath and waited. Then, suddenly, the lights flicked back on, and Connor was gone, vanished into thin air.

CHAPTER 13

Where did he go? I gripped the sides of my chair until my fingernails dug into the wood. My stomach twisted and the tiny hairs on my arms stood on end, but I didn't have long to overcome my shock. As soon as the lights were back on, everything in the cabin roared to life.

The page about school fires popped back up on my laptop. The opening song for *WALL·E* blared on the TV down the hall. An alarm sounded in Mom's office. The washer and dryer whirred and banged. A Bluetooth speaker in the bathroom blasted jazz music. There was so much noise, I couldn't pinpoint where all of it was coming from. Most concerning was the shrill beep of every smoke and carbon monoxide detector in the cabin.

I bolted from my seat then ran out of the kitchen and down the hallway, pausing briefly outside Mom's office. The alarm coming from this room was the same one that had gone off when we'd been watching the movie. I knew it had something to do with the research facility. It struck me that the electronics had worked just fine until I'd started having problems with my classmates. That's when things had started going haywire at Mom's work, too, and with Seas the Day's internal server. Regardless of what Mom thought, I knew it was connected.

The ruckus of every appliance, every electronic device, turning on at once made it hard to think. And was it my imagination, or did I smell smoke?

I followed my nose back into the kitchen. The microwave drew my attention first. It was whirring and beeping loudly, and the glass was illuminated by an interior light. There was also smoke rising around it. It took me a minute to realize that the smoke was coming not from the microwave itself, but from the stovetop beneath it. All four electric burners were bright red, and a hot pad was draped across the largest one. My first thought was to remove the smoldering pad from the burner, but as soon as I got close, it burst into flames.

Smoke engulfed me. I broke into a coughing fit as I changed course and went for the fire extinguisher my parents kept beneath the sink. My hands trembled as I pulled the pin, aimed the hose, and squeezed the handle. The fire was out in a matter of seconds. But just like with my phone, I couldn't get the stove to respond to my touch. I jammed the buttons over and over, but it wouldn't turn off. Neither would the microwave.

I didn't know what to do. It was pure chaos and whatever was happening, I knew the electronics in our cabin were not designed for this much energy to be flowing through them. I'd dealt with the hot pad, but how long before something else burst into flame? A socket? Wiring in the wall? I thought about running from room to room and unplugging everything before a radio or lamp spontaneously combusted, but that would take time.

I threw my hands up to cover my ears. If I could just make the noise stop, maybe I could think clearly. But I hadn't had any luck so far controlling the electronic devices. It hit me that if I couldn't turn off all the noise, my next best option was to get away from it. I darted through the house and out the front door.

As soon as I was a safe distance from the house, I tried calling Mom. It went directly to voicemail. My fingers shook as I clicked end and tried Dad's number next. He picked up on the second ring. "Hello?"

"Dad!"

"Hello?" Dad said a second time.

"Dad! Dad, it's me." I was practically choking on the panic rising in my throat.

"Must be a bad connection," he mumbled. "If you can hear me, call me back."

I could hear him just fine. That wasn't the problem. "Wait!" I begged. "Please, don't hang up!"

Click.

I immediately tried again. This time, I couldn't get the call to connect even though I had plenty of bars. Texting failed me, too. Each time I madly typed a message, *Mom come home!* and *I need you!* a red exclamation point popped up. I went through everyone on my favorites list. I even tried calling Aunt Julie who lived on the east coast, all the way on the other side of the continent. Nothing would go through. Nothing. Not even a call to 911. I had no idea how I'd explain my emergency if someone had picked up, but that was the least of my concerns.

Just when I gave up on my phone and shoved it back in my pocket, it dinged. *Yes!* Thinking one of my texts had finally gone through and I was getting a response, I whipped it back out. When I saw that the sender was Mara, I flinched. I couldn't get the image of her in the school photo out of my head. I still couldn't quite believe it, but the Mara I knew had been dead for a hundred years.

You're not safe. Come find us. We'll protect you.

I didn't know who to trust or where I'd be safer—here where Connor (or his spirit?) might be lingering, or somewhere else. Connor had been sitting in my kitchen one moment and was gone the next. He was in the photo with the other students, but he wasn't with them now. At least, he hadn't ever acted like he was a part of the class, and they hadn't mentioned him before, either. Harold said the thirteenth child was most likely responsible for the school fire. Did that mean Connor was responsible for their deaths? Was it also him who nearly caused the fire in my kitchen just now?

I tried sending Mom another text. Then I tried calling. It was still no use. Whatever was interfering with the electronics inside the cabin was interfering with my phone, too. My only hope of contacting someone in the outside world now was through Mara.

Against my better judgment, I responded to her text: *Where?*

You know where.

No, my gut protested. I knew Mara meant the one place she kept sending me to—the ruins and the tiny graveyard. It was the last place I wanted to go. But it didn't feel safe to step back inside the cabin, not with Connor setting off all the electronics and trying to kill me the same way he had the other students.

It wasn't like I totally trusted Mara and the others now that I knew Connor was the thirteenth student, but maybe they could help me reach my mom. It was too far to walk to the research facility, but I could walk to the graveyard. My phone dinged again:

We can help. Just come.

Not knowing what else to do, I set off. The snow melted enough this afternoon that I didn't need snowshoes. Still, as I plodded along in my fluffy "first day of school" snow boots, it made me sick to see them on my feet. Everything that had anything to do with me meeting my classmates in real life now seemed, I don't know . . . tainted or something.

As I went down the path, I swore I could see faces in every shadow. It seemed like each rock or tree provided the perfect cover for someone or something to jump out at me. The thing was, I wasn't 100 percent convinced that fleeing from Connor was the right choice, not considering who I was running to.

I felt something brushing against my pants and thought it was boney fingers scratching at my legs. I screeched and leaped forward, only to look back and see that I'd passed through a patch of twigs. My eyes darted around the forest—up and down, side to side. I was as afraid that another branch would tumble down from above as I was of being attacked by someone lurking behind a tree. My breaths were coming too quickly; I didn't feel like I was getting enough air. Then there was my head. It felt heavy and woolly. I wasn't thinking clearly.

I wanted to be calm and calculating, but my fear and anxiety were getting the better of me. Instead of feeling in control, I was panicking. So, I stopped in my tracks.

Dad taught me the three-three-three method for grounding

myself when my worries got too big. I used it now. I searched for three things I could see: a light gray cumulus cloud, a pinecone, a muddy snowbank. I listened to three noises: the murmur of the river in the distance, a water drip falling from a branch, the wind whistling through the woods. I touched three things: the rough bark on a tree, a cold smooth rock, and then the warmth of my own cheek.

When I felt calmer, I began walking again. Despite everything, I was proud of myself for getting ahold of my fears. It took every last bit of my determination, but I even made it past the ruins without falling apart.

Then, before I knew it, I had arrived at the tiny graveyard.

"Okay, I'm here." I announced myself. I spun in circles. Where were my classmates? Would they show themselves at last?

My phone dinged with another text from Mara.

Welcome, Lucy! We're so glad you decided to join us. We're going to have so much fun.

Fun? It's not like I'd expected to run into their open arms, or anything. But I'd been scared out of my mind, and Mara wasn't concerned. She wasn't sympathetic or offering me refuge. If anything, the text felt mocking. My phone buzzed and vibrated in my hand again. This time it was Jamie.

So much fun that you'll never want to leave.

Ever.

I heard laughter coming from the forest. This time, the sound was unmistakable.

I group-texted Mara and Jamie: *Why are you hiding? This isn't funny.*

Mara responded immediately: *It isn't supposed to be funny. It isn't a game.*

The back of my neck tingled. I spun on my heels, certain someone had blown a hot breath across my skin.

No one was there.

In an instant, I knew I'd made a terrible mistake by coming here. They weren't going to help me. They'd never intended to.

I glared directly at Mara's headstone. "Stop messing with me. You said you could protect me." Then I let my gaze bounce from headstone to headstone.

That's when I saw it.

It had been buried by snow the last time I was here, but there was indeed a thirteenth headstone. Broken into pieces, the smaller part was still upright, but the larger portion of the marker had been knocked flat. Its beveled edges were barely peeking out of the snow.

Curiosity got the better of me. I knelt in the slush and then, using my bare hand, cleared the remaining flakes from the face of the headstone. The snow brushed away easily. It must've fallen in the recent storm. If it had been through the deep freeze of winter, it wouldn't be so simple to remove. I fully expected to find Connor's name engraved in the stone. He had to be the thirteenth child, but I still wanted confirmation that it was him. That he was the one who'd set fire to the schoolhouse long ago and was now creating the electrical interference at my home.

What I saw came as such a shock, however, it curdled my blood. I read and reread the stone. The epitaph wasn't for Connor. Instead, in bold letters it spelled out: LUCY BELL-RODRIGUEZ.

I dug my fingers into the channels running through the granite. It wasn't possible. *This* had to be a trick. But the engraving didn't budge. It was rigid and cold. It felt just like the engravings on the other twelve markers.

Then I saw the dates.

OCTOBER 21, 2012–APRIL 13, 2025

Today's date was April 12. According to the marker, I would die tomorrow.

For a moment I just stared at my headstone, feeling weirdly detached from the world around me. It was like I was watching a movie, and this was happening to someone else. The forest around me faded away.

Glowing orbs appeared like giant fireflies in the woods. The sound of their coldhearted laughter grew louder. The lights drew closer and began to form a circle around me. Then my phone dinged once more.

I told you it wasn't a game.

I sprang to my feet, then stumbled over myself as I broke into a run. The forest was murky now that the sun was almost down. I saw shadows everywhere I looked, and the drop in temperature had turned the slush to ice. I was unsteady enough on my feet. The lack of light and the slippery ground made it even worse.

Every few feet I glanced over my shoulder to see if I was being followed. The orbs grew smaller in the distance until they disappeared entirely. Not that it made me feel any safer. They were ghosts. They didn't have to play by ordinary rules.

Now that I knew my life was in danger, I couldn't just ignore the ruins as I passed by, either. This time, I strained my eyes to search for figures in the windows, for more light. I found neither. But I perked up my ears when I heard a soft crack. I quickened my speed, even though I was already running dangerously fast on the slick ground.

Another crack hit my ears. It sounded closer this time. It sounded like a twig snapping. Someone or something was chasing me. Just as I cleared the ruins and reentered a heavily wooded portion of the path, my right boot landed on a patch of ice and my feet flew out from under me. I landed flat on my back.

I heard rustling again. Whatever it was, it was gaining on me, and I thought, *This is it. I'm caught. I'm going to die.*

But when I turned my head, instead of a glowing orb or ghostly figure, I came face-to-face with a furry marmot. His black eyes looked almost as frightened as I felt. If I hadn't been so terrified, I might've laughed. Instead, I rolled over and pulled myself back up as the large rodent scampered off.

I'd gone down hard, and everything hurt. Thankfully, though, I wasn't injured. As I started down the path again, I was still in a hurry, but I was more cautious about it. Ice was impossible to see in the shadows, and I didn't want to take another fall. The thing was, I had no idea how I might die, only that the head- stone predicted that I would. And soon. If I wasn't careful, I'd be the cause of my own death.

CHAPTER 14

Our cabin was pitch-black and silent as I slipped inside. I wanted to breathe a sigh of relief, but I couldn't. Not yet. Just because I didn't see or hear a threat didn't mean it wasn't there. Deciding it was worth the risk to get rid of the darkness, I raced around the house, flipping on every light switch I passed. When nothing attacked me, I still couldn't relax. Instead, I ran my fingers through my hair and paced up and down the hallways.

What could I do? Mom still wasn't home, and Dad was in California. I thought maybe since the electronics had gone silent, my phone would work now. I whipped it out, and Mara's text was still on the screen—as if I needed a reminder.

I told you it wasn't a game.

It wasn't a game. My life really was in danger. My breath quivered in my throat, and I felt like throwing my phone at the wall. I didn't, of course. But I did shove it back in my pocket when, like before, I found that none of my texts or calls would go through.

I couldn't just hang around waiting to die, though. If there was something I could do, anything to prevent it from happening, I needed to figure out what that was.

I had an idea, so I dashed to the kitchen to retrieve my laptop. I barely paused at the kitchen table, remembering how Connor had been sitting there not long before. And how when I'd discovered his true identity, he'd just vanished into thin air.

I quickly snatched my laptop from the table, then went directly to my room and shut the door—*as if that could protect me.*

Still, if I couldn't call anyone, maybe I could get an email to go through. But the moment I flipped the laptop open, a video chat invitation popped up on my screen. Just like when I'd seen the dates on the headstone—make that *my* headstone—I went numb again.

There was no hiding from it, though. No hiding from *them.* My hand shook as I clicked to join. Twelve boxes appeared, a smiling face in each one. The click of Mara's tongue was audible through the speakers. "Why did you leave so soon?" she asked. "You know you can't escape us, right? There's been an empty grave for far too long, but now you will be the one to fill it."

I caught a glance of the pale, horror-stricken image of the girl my camera was projecting and did a double take. I didn't recognize her at first, but the girl was me. It was me, wearing the old-fashioned dress again. Lacy collar. Buttons down the front. My hair in braids. The video stream matched the reflection of me that I'd seen in the hand mirror I'd found at the ruins. I got a good long look and was horrified by what I saw. Worse, the image didn't shimmer and disappear this time. It stayed on my screen. Like the nightmare I'd found myself in, it wasn't going away.

"Why me?" I asked.

"Because we like you," Josephine said sweetly. Something wicked flashed in her eyes, though. It looked like . . . hunger.

I recoiled. "Ms. Grant, are you there?" I called out in desperation. "Will you help me, please?" I knew I was grasping at straws. Ms. Grant had never been responsive before. Still, turning to an adult felt like the right thing to do. It felt like what I was supposed to do, anyway.

Jamie laughed and I sunk deeper into despair. "There is no Ms. Grant," he said. "Well, there was . . . but she's no longer with us."

Who's been assigning all the homework, then? And keeping the class on track?

As if Jamie could hear my thoughts, he added, "Oh, wait, here

111

you go . . ." A message popped up in the chat box. Ms. Grant: *Class canceled for all of eternity.*

"Better?" Jamie asked.

I turned my head, so I didn't have to see his smirk. There had to be another way. Did Dad have a personal locater beacon or a flare somewhere in all his outdoor gear?

"You know we're in control, don't you, Lucy? No matter how you try to get help. We will stop you," Mara said.

For once, I knew she was telling the truth. Even if I found the beacon, they'd make sure it didn't work. And a flare? There would have to be someone looking to see it. It might work somewhere close to civilization, but here? Regardless, it was bad enough that they wanted me dead. I didn't have to sit here and take their abuse.

I slammed my laptop shut at the same time the cabin went dark again. A few seconds later, the lights flickered back on, and they were there. My classmates stood in front of me, shoulder to shoulder, spread across the length of my room. Their clothes were scorched and covered with ash. There was a hole in Josephine's dress. My stomach turned when I saw a patch of her flesh. It didn't have a normal, healthy glow. It was shiny red in some places and blackened in others. But their faces were even more repulsive. Layers of skin were peeling off and falling away. Jamie's right cheekbone was protruding from an open wound. I gagged as a putrid smell, like burning hair and decay, flooded the room.

Mara's blistered lips twisted into a sardonic smile. "Soon," she said. "Soon, there will be thirteen of us again."

I shuddered and dropped my gaze. When the lights suddenly flickered back off, I knew it was time to move. I sucked in my breath and mustered the courage to break free from the fear that held me rooted in place. As I sprang forward, I felt their hands grabbing for me in the dark. Their touch was light, but their fingers were so very cold as they brushed across my cheeks and skimmed my arms. I kept going and slipped free of their grasp. I fumbled for the knob, twisted it, and then burst through the door just as the lights came back on.

I didn't know what was happening with the electricity. It could've been Connor causing the disturbances, or it could have been the other twelve. Either way, my gut told me the dead children were behind it. If only I could find a way to cut them off from their power source. That's when I remembered the breaker box on the side of the house. I went out the front door, turned the corner, then threw the cover on the box open the second I reached it. I didn't know nearly as much about electricity as Mom, but I knew enough to know the circuit breaker box was where all the wiring from inside the cabin was connected to White Pine's power grid. Mom had shown me how to cut the power in case of emergency. No doubt, this *was* an emergency.

I quickly located the main circuit switch and flipped it to the left. Immediately, a ZAP ran through my fingers. It tingled up my arm, and every cell of my body screamed in pain. The electrical charge made my finger muscles tight. It locked them in place. I couldn't break contact with the switch. The last clear thought I had before everything went black was that if I couldn't let go, it would kill me.

CHAPTER 15

CONNOR
APRIL 12, 1925

White Pine, Alaska, was far removed from the boom of jazz, electricity, and automobiles sweeping the country. Connor rose before dawn and tended to the fire in his family's tiny, hand-hewed log cabin. He warmed milk in a kettle for his baby brother, Finn. While it was heating, he found a day-old biscuit for himself.

There were several chores he'd need to complete before school, and with the ice breaking up on the river, he hoped to fish afterward. In fact, he couldn't stop thinking about going fishing. While he swept the cabin floor and then chopped wood with an ax, he fantasized about the fish fry he and his family would have that night. As early as he'd awoken, his parents had risen before him. His dad had taken the wagon to Fairbanks for the first time this year. He would return with butter and onions, among other supplies. The fresh-caught salmon would sizzle and pop in the butter as it fried in the pan above the fire. Connor's mouth watered just thinking about it.

When his mother returned from the barn, she was carrying a basket of freshly laid eggs. It had been a harsh winter, but Connor had been attentive to the chickens, scooping out and cleaning the coop regularly, and adding extra layers of straw. Most had survived.

After pecking his mother's cheek with a kiss and patting his brother on the head, he left for school. He brought both his fishing rod and book bag with him.

The illness that claimed the lives of two of his siblings had spared Connor but left him small and weak for his age. His scrawny size, pale skin, and bright red hair made him a target for the other students. "How do you tell the difference between Connor and a matchstick?" Mara would ask. Then she'd cackle and say, "You don't."

It didn't help any that Connor was assigned the job of cleaning the schoolhouse chimney because of his small size. He could more easily fit into the cramped space, but he hated climbing the narrow flue and scrubbing out the soot and ash. Not only did he scrape and bruise his elbows and knees, but he also found being confined inside the brick channel terrifying. Each time he completed the work, he came out choking and gasping for air. His aversion to the task fueled further ridicule.

"What's the matter?" Jamie would feign concern. "You'd think a matchstick would feel right at home in a place made for lighting fires."

Fortunately, the chimney only needed a good sweeping every few months. Unfortunately, it was overdue.

Connor spent the school day trying to stay out of the crosshairs of the other students. Every so often he'd glance toward the back of the one-room schoolhouse at the fishing rod tucked behind his leather schoolbag. Unlike the numerous rods he'd fashioned from sticks, this one was special. It had been a Christmas present from his parents. Last fall his dad had traded a large portion of their crops for a pole made from bamboo. The bamboo was lighter and sleeker than anything he'd used before. Connor couldn't wait to try it out. He could only imagine how far he'd be able to cast his fishing line with the new rod.

When Ms. Grant called Connor to her desk, sweeping the chimney was the last thing on his mind. Therefore, when she said, "Connor, you must stay after school today to clean the flue," it took him a moment to register what she was asking. Cleaning the flue would eat up precious daylight hours. It would eat up precious *fishing* hours. Connor was caught so off guard that he forgot himself and blurted out, "But Ms. Grant, please, can't it wait?"

The teacher had gone back to her stack of papers. It was rare that her statements were challenged by a student. Her head whipped up, and with a stern look in her eye, she said, "Young man, if your hands weren't required for this particular task, it would be the ruler for you. Now, you will stay after school today and clean the flue, and I don't want to hear another word about it."

Connor swallowed hard, then said, "Yes, ma'am." After all, swollen hands wouldn't do for fishing, either.

The day had dragged on before. Now that Connor had nothing to look forward to, and instead had something to dread, it was positively glacial. When the end of the school day finally came and Ms. Grant dismissed the students, everyone else sprang for the door. Connor shrank in his seat, waiting for the schoolhouse to empty. Jamie deliberately bumped into him on his way down the aisle. "Watch it, Matchstick."

As usual, Connor didn't react, but in his stomach, there was a pit of rage and frustration, mixed with humiliation. It only grew as he glanced back and forth between his fishing rod and the fireplace. His stomach growled at the thought of the fish fry that wouldn't be.

On previous occasions, Ms. Grant had supervised while Connor squeezed into the tiny space above the firebox, through the throat of the chimney, and then clambered up the flue. So, he was surprised when she began packing up her items after the others had left.

"Ms. Grant—" Connor started, then bit his tongue when he remembered she'd threatened him with a ruler once already for questioning her.

"You know the procedure by now. I'll check your work tomorrow before I light the morning fire. I expect to find not a trace of ash or soot."

"Yes, ma'am."

As soon as Connor was alone, he retrieved the tools from the shed and then returned to the chimney. He started with the broom and dustbin. There were tiny sparks of red mixed in with the black ash as he swept the firebox clean. When he scooped the residue into the dustbin and then went to transfer the pile into a pail, a hot ember escaped. It landed on his wrist and singed his skin. The pain wasn't severe, but it was enough to bring out the emotions that had been boiling in his stomach.

Connor threw the dustbin to the ground. It clanged and clattered as it skidded across the hardwood floor. It wasn't fair. He should be testing out his new rod, not stuck here burning himself while doing a chore he loathed. Because he was the smallest in the class, he was forced to do the job nobody else wanted to do.

It wasn't that Connor was averse to hard work. There was

satisfaction in building a fence, harvesting a crop, or even cleaning a stable—where the fruits of one's labor were visible to all. But this? Ms. Grant said she'd check his work, but even if she lowered herself to the floor and peered up the long, black hole, would she be able to tell if the buildup had been brushed and scraped away, or would she just see darkness? Connor knew it would be the latter.

Now that he'd cleaned the firebox, who would know if he didn't finish the job? He knew it needed to be done, but why couldn't he complete it on a day when his dad wasn't bringing home onions and butter, and when it hadn't been months since he'd eaten salmon fresh from the river?

Connor knew he was alone. Still, he glanced about the schoolhouse to see if anyone was watching before quickly doing what was necessary to make it look like he'd finished the job. He found a patch of snow outside to douse the embers in the pail and he returned all the tools to the shed. He told himself that he'd stay behind on an upcoming school day and complete sweeping the flue just as soon as he had a chance. Today, however, he retrieved his schoolbag and fishing rod and didn't look back.

CHAPTER 16

When the gray, fuzzy edges of my vision came into focus, I found myself staring into Connor's hazel eyes. His face was inches above mine. The dull throbbing in my head made it difficult to remember anything, but then, slowly, things started to come back to me.

I thought this boy was my friend . . . for a little while, at least. But he wasn't. Connor was . . . dead. I hurriedly scooted away from him on my elbows until there was enough room between us that I could sit up. My head spun as I rose. "Did you . . . did you pull me away from the switch?"

Connor nodded timidly, then asked, "Are you okay?"

I was far from okay. I shot back, "Who are you, really?" It came out more like an accusation than a question, but I didn't trust him. It was impossible, considering the truth I'd uncovered. He'd been in the photo with the other students. They had all lived and died a hundred years ago.

His shoulders drooped. I could tell my words hit him hard, and he shrank deeper inside his too-large coat. He looked away and didn't answer.

"They were your classmates first," I said, not letting up. "You're the thirteenth student."

A tiny part of me still clung to the hope that it wasn't true. That it was all a big misunderstanding. That we'd get past this somehow and I'd sew him that pouch and we'd go fishing, and life would go on.

But Connor kept his head turned. He didn't deny it.

"Is it your fault the others died?" I asked.

"Yes," he said, still not meeting my eyes.

His response shook me to the core. He was so matter-of-fact. It was chilling. He'd just admitted responsibility for the death of twelve children, and he'd barely blinked an eye. I didn't like being so near to him. So close to a . . . a murderer. He was on his knees, and I was sitting. The few inches he hovered above me suddenly felt threatening. I clambered to my feet.

Mom had always been dismissive of ghost stories, and I think her skepticism wore off on me. I'd never really been a big fan of them or fairy tales. Still, I'd read a few. What I could recall was that the ghosts were often trapped between this world and the next because of some sort of unfinished business. Be it revenge, guilt, or unfulfilled promises, the ghosts couldn't move on until they addressed whatever was keeping them here on earth.

Connor also rose to his feet, but his eyes never left my face.

If that were true and Connor was doomed to haunt White Pine, then he might have as much reason as the others, maybe more, to want me dead. Maybe there were rules for how he went about filling his empty grave. What if the reason he rescued me from electrocution was because I needed to die a certain way?

I kept my eyes trained on the slight boy, and his gaze stayed fixed on me. He'd seemed so gentle and kind before. Could he really be a murderer?

At last, Connor reached his hand toward me.

I flinched.

"Please, you must—"

He didn't get a chance to finish because right then, we both heard the sound of tires crushing the gravel in the circle drive.

I didn't hesitate. I ducked away from Connor and ran toward the front of the house and the arriving vehicle. Whatever Connor thought I "must" do—Give in? Go with him to my grave?—I wasn't going to stick around to find out.

I really hoped it was Mom coming home. I practically fantasized about seeing her silver SUV again. So, when I found a green truck pulling up instead, I stumbled over my own feet. And even though the face behind the wheel was familiar, I stopped running toward it.

When Harold saw me, he waved.

This time, it was me who didn't return the gesture. I would rather have seen any other living person on the planet just then. Even Bailey Henderson.

But—to be fair, he was *living*.

After a brief pause, I started moving toward the vehicle again. Sure, the old man creeped me out, but it's not like I had any better options. I reached the truck just as it rolled to a stop. I flung the passenger door open, then before the security guard could say a word, I hopped inside the cab and shut it behind me. "Can you take me to my mom?" I blurted.

Harold's jaw tensed, then he said, "I can do that." While he put the truck back in gear and it started moving again, he added, "As a matter of fact, that's why I'm here. Dr. Rodriguez sent me to check on you. She said your dad received a strange call from you and then neither of them was able to reach you by phone."

I whipped my head toward him. "Why didn't she come herself?" I was kind of hurt that Mom had sent Harold. I wanted to think that if she'd knew what I'd been going through, she would've dropped everything and come running.

"She would have, but she's busy putting out fires at the lab."

I drew back slightly in my seat. Were things really that bad where Mom was at? I doubted her work problems could rival the literal fire I'd put out in the kitchen, not to mention my near-death by electrocution, but it did make me wonder. Were the students wreaking as much havoc with the research facility equipment as they had at the cabin?

The security guard gave me a measuring glance out of the corner of his eye. "Everything all right?"

The answer to that question was, of course, no.

I smoothed back my hair. I could only imagine how frightened and frazzled I looked. I mean, I didn't just *look* it. I *was* frightened and frazzled. Still, I didn't know where to begin explaining the situation. After an awkward pause, I shrugged before lifting my chin. "I will be."

"Did you return to the school?"

His sudden interest in my life took me by surprise. During my two previous encounters with the security guard, he'd been quiet and reserved. Now he was projecting a nervous sort of energy. It made me uneasy. His voice sounded more strained than gruff. The veins on the backs of his hands bulged. His fingers gripped the steering wheel too tightly.

A few minutes later, I realized we were traveling in the wrong direction. When I'd visited the facility before, Mom had taken a right when we'd reached the paved road. Harold had taken a left.

"Where are we going?" I asked. I tried to mask the panic in my voice.

Harold fell silent and his gaze shifted back and forth between me and the road.

Oh no! This was bad. I never should've gotten in the truck with him. I just . . . I thought it was a way out of danger. But I'd been wrong.

My heartbeat kicked up again and I felt sick. I scanned the inside of the truck, trying to figure out what I was in for. At least nothing in the cab seemed out of the ordinary. No knives or ropes, or other menacing objects. But then the truck went over a bump in the road and a pair of tools came sliding out from under the bench seat in the back of the cab.

I tilted my head at the sight of the hammer and chisel. A stencil had also slid into view. The letters *L*, *U*, and *C* were now visible. I could feel the blood draining from my face as I thought about how I'd dipped my fingers in the new epitaph on the old, broken headstone. The thirteenth headstone.

It was then that I began to get my bearings. I knew exactly where Harold was taking me. Back to the empty grave. The one with my name on it.

"You're helping them!" I cried out. "You chiseled my name into the stone. That was you! The tree branch that nearly crushed me . . . was that you, too?"

For a second, it seemed Harold couldn't meet my eyes. Then something in him hardened. He bore into me with his gaze and laughed scornfully. "It's nothing personal," he said.

The edge to his voice was chilling and my heart pounded against my rib cage.

"Why do you think we have no children in White Pine?" Harold asked, but it was obvious he didn't expect an answer. "Ever since I was a boy, the families who moved here have been frightened away. My own wife and child left because of the students. They tormented my son. They crashed Sam's train sets and smashed his fingers in the cupboards."

I recalled the toys I'd seen in his cabin and felt a twinge of pity—not for Harold, but for his child.

"They told my son his great-uncle, my dad's brother, was a murderer."

Wait. When I was at his cabin, Harold said his dad's brother had gone to White Pine Secondary. If his uncle was the thirteenth student, that meant . . . Harold was Connor's nephew. Connor was a murderer, and they were *family*.

"My wife didn't believe our son at first," Harold continued. "Then the phone calls started. She'd find Sam talking to someone on the old handset in the kitchen late at night. Someone named Mara, who kept telling Sam to come into the forest. She promised they'd 'have so much fun.' The thing was, the phone calls kept coming, even when my wife unplugged the phone. She packed their bags after that. She begged me to come with them. But, you see, White Pine is more than my home. My family sacrificed more than blood and tears for this land. I couldn't up and abandon their legacy. Now Sam is a grown man with children of his own. But do you think they ever visit?"

What was Harold saying? Did he think helping the students was going to fix everything? There were so many things I didn't understand. But I was certain that Harold would see to it that the students were successful. Which, unless I managed to escape soon, meant I was going to die.

There was a snowbank up ahead and a curve in the road. Maybe . . .

I unclipped my seat belt.

"What are you doing?" Harold snarled as I grabbed the cold, metal door handle and yanked. It didn't open. As I fumbled with the lock, Harold grabbed hold of my coat jacket. The truck swerved and slowed just as we reached the bend.

The second I managed to pop the latch, I yanked the handle again. The door flew open. Harold still had a grip on my sleeve. The stitches ripped apart as I launched out of the seat. At the last second, the fabric slipped from his grasp. Midair, I folded myself into a ball and aimed for the softest landing.

My right shoulder hit the ground first. My arms and legs

came untucked. I bounced and rolled. Then bounced and rolled again. I didn't know which way was up. Each time I skidded across the icy embankment, pain radiated through my body. When I finally came to a stop, everything hurt so badly, I wasn't sure I could get up.

That was, until I heard the screech of tires and saw Harold's break lights illuminating a short distance ahead. I had to get up. My life depended on it.

As I rose, a shooting pain traveled from my ankle up my entire leg. Still, I could put some weight on it, which made me think it was sprained, not broken. The way my body had jolted and twisted upon impact, I was lucky I hadn't been hurt worse, but still . . . I groaned and muttered a swear word. An injury was the last thing I needed.

Steeling myself against the pain, I began hobbling toward the forest. I didn't dare look back, but I knew I was being followed. Harold was old, but he'd lived an active life. He still moved swiftly despite his age. The length of his stride alone gave him an advantage over my shorter steps. Considering I couldn't run with my throbbing ankle, my best bet was to find somewhere to hide.

Of course, hiding wouldn't be easy, either. Although there were patches of soil and areas where underbrush was peeking through, most of the ground was still covered in snow. It was nearly impossible to not leave tracks. Also, the trees were sparser here than they were near the ruins and the tiny graveyard. But I'd have to be out of my mind to go that direction—toward my own grave.

"Lucy!" Harold called after me. "There's nowhere for you to go."

I spotted the river a short distance ahead. In the areas where it cut through the land, I knew there would be more boulders and vegetation, more places to find cover.

I scrambled down a steep portion of the embankment, and quickly lost my footing. For a terrifying second, I barreled toward the icy, cold water. After a few feet, I regained some traction and then skidded to a stop at the bottom. From there, I could see that the other side had thick trees and deep, rocky crevices. Places I could easily slip into. My side, however, was barren. If I stayed here, I'd not only be out in the open, but I'd also be trapped against the river.

Harold was still calling my name, and he was gaining on me. I continued to ignore him and looked for a place to cross. The water was flowing freely, rushing even, as the spring melt was trickling in. If only I'd been a few weeks, or even a few days, earlier, it would've been frozen enough to safely get to the other side. Now it would be risky . . .

Putting as little weight as possible on my tender ankle, I

slowly picked my way across by stepping from rock to rock. The stone faces were slick, and several times, I nearly slid in. By the time I got close to the other side, Harold was cresting the riverbank behind me. The ridge was steeper where he stood than where I'd descended, and his voice echoed down to me. "You can't keep running, Lucy. Please, try to understand," he pleaded. "I have to set things right."

I leaped across the last stretch of the river. When I landed, my bad leg crumbled beneath me, and I fell to my knees on the rocky bank.

"It has to stop," Harold pleaded. "The students are even stronger now. They feed off the energy the facility produces. It'll only get worse, and it won't end. Not until the empty grave is filled."

I peered up at him from the place where I'd fallen.

"It was my family that brought the curse upon this land and our homestead. That's why I must set it right. I don't want to help them, but I have no other choice."

Harold looked anguished, but I didn't feel even a shred of sympathy for him. I narrowed my gaze, and that's when I noticed something else—a shock of red just beyond his right shoulder, and the shadow of a thin figure creeping up behind him.

The look of surprise on my face must've alerted Harold

because he spun around. What happened next occurred so quickly, I couldn't trust my own eyes. There was a scuffle on the ridge. Harold lost his footing, then tumbled backward.

I didn't want to watch the old man fall, so I looked away. When I heard a splash, I turned my gaze to the swift-moving area of the river where he would have landed. I didn't see anything but rivulets of water with little whitecaps. There was no doubt in my mind that the current had dragged him away.

Alarmingly, when my gaze traveled up the ridge, I saw that Connor was also gone. Was he coming for me next? I had to get away, but where could I go? Was anywhere safe? I could try slipping into the woods or making a break for it, then return home. But I was terrified that no matter where I went, Connor, or the others, would find me.

"Lucy?"

The sound of my name being spoken directly behind me made me go rigid. It was all I could do to bite back a scream. Apparently, it was already too late to run and hide. My heart was racing as I slowly swiveled around to face Connor. "What . . . what do you want?" My voice quavered.

He held something in his hand and was extending it toward me. "I think you might find these useful."

I opened my palm to receive a set of keys. As soon as I curled my fingers around them, Connor vanished. Like before, I could feel his presence lingering even though I could no longer see him. I remained very still. After a little while, the sensation went away, and I could breathe more easily again.

I tried to work through what had just happened. Had Connor really pushed Harold over the ridge? Why did that shock me? I mean, he'd admitted to killing the twelve other students, hadn't he? A shiver ran through me, thinking of how callous he'd seemed when I asked him about it. If Harold was right and the empty grave had to be filled for this to end, it should be him who filled it, not me. The way I saw it, we were enemies in this. Then, why was he helping me? Unless . . . it was a trick? I turned my attention to the large, silver ring with several keys dangling from it. I'd seen it recently, hanging from the ignition in Harold's truck. Connor had given me Harold's keys.

Was he expecting me to crash? Was he just helping me along on my path to an untimely death? Or . . . was the truck now my only hope for escape? If I went far from the graveyard, would I be safe? Maybe I could find Mom and we could leave White Pine before its inhabitants did me in.

There were so many things that could go wrong behind the wheel of a truck. Yet, a short time later, I found myself sitting in the driver's seat, turning the keys over in the ignition. The engine roared to life. For a moment, I did nothing more than wait to see if something or someone would possess the vehicle the way they had my phone and household electronics. If I was sure of one thing, it was that I had no idea how any of this worked. If my classmates wanted to drive me off the road, I imagined they could. Nothing would surprise me anymore.

When no poltergeist took over the instrument panel, I decided to give it a shot. I knew the basics but had never driven before and was years away from getting my license. If it wasn't my best chance of reaching Mom, it would be out of the question. At least there wouldn't be another vehicle on the road. I fiddled around with the shifter until I figured out how to get it into drive, then pressed my foot to the gas.

My touch was too soft at first (no movement) and then too hard (the truck jerked forward) until I found the sweet spot in the middle. The steering wasn't difficult. I thanked my years of things on wheels (skateboards, bicycles, and go-karts), for that. After a few minutes, I was cruising down the road at a slow but steady fifteen miles per hour. The ghosts could catch me at any speed if they wanted, and it was still much faster than walking.

I pressed down harder on the accelerator, gradually increasing my speed as I tried to outrun this horrible nightmare.

CHAPTER 17

CONNOR
APRIL 12, 1925

As soon as White Pine Secondary was out of sight, it was out of mind. Connor could think of nothing other than the flowing river and the prospect of a fish fry for dinner. He skipped along, enjoying the rays of sunlight breaking through the pine needles overhead. His brother had been too young the previous season for anything other than their mother's milk. He'd never had fish fresh from the river. Connor imagined how he'd strip the buttery flakes of meat from the fragile fish bones to share with Baby Finn. He could practically hear his coos of delight already.

Connor was shaken from his daydream by the sound of a snapping twig. He froze. "Who's there?"

Connor tried to swallow his fear, but it was impossible. This time of year, the bears would be coming out of hibernation.

He heard another snap and immediately dropped flat to his stomach. The ground was still frozen and the cold seeped through his clothing. A patch of ice scraped his left cheek as he attempted to lie still while protecting his head with his hands. Normally a bear would move on, but the salmon weren't running yet, and the grizzlies were hungry.

Connor didn't lift his head until he heard muffled snickering. His classmates were all there, and they had him surrounded. Mara, Jamie, Josephine, Henry, George, Elizabeth, Lillian, Walter, Annabel, Ruth, Peter, and Marie. It was the first day of warmer weather. While he'd stayed behind to clean the chimney, the other students hadn't wandered far and had been playing outdoors. Connor felt the familiar pang of not belonging.

"Afraid of something, Matchstick?" Jamie sneered.

"Don't worry," Mara said with false sincerity. "It's bulls that are angered by red, not bears."

Henry held two fingers to each side of his head, shaping them like horns. Then he scuffed and scraped one foot on the ground before charging toward Connor.

Connor scrambled to his feet and barely sidestepped Henry's attack.

"Toro! Toro!" Mara cheered.

Henry pivoted and continued to act like a bull, scraping his foot once more and then snorting.

Connor kept his eyes on Henry while trying to back away, but there was no escaping the circle the students had formed.

Mara crept up behind him. "What's this?" she asked, and snagged the bamboo rod from his pack.

Connor reeled on her. "Give it back!"

Mara held it high above his reach. "I saw you staring at it all day. Is it new?"

When he came close, she tossed the rod to Henry. Henry dropped the raging-bull routine and studied the rod. He whistled.

"Please?" Connor begged, and walked forward with his hands outstretched. "Please give it back."

"What? This?" Jamie asked, then tossed it over Connor's head to Ruth. Their game continued with Connor in the middle of the circle. They all joined in, playing keep-away with his rod until it was passed to Josephine.

Josephine hesitated, only for a second, but long enough for everyone to think she might take pity on Connor and return his prized possession. Unfortunately for Connor, Mara was, as usual, a step ahead. She snatched the rod from Josephine's hands and before he could do anything to stop her, she snapped it over her knee. The bamboo fell to the ground in two jagged pieces.

"Oops," Mara said. "I guess the game is over."

Connor fell to his knees and gathered the pieces of his rod. He gripped one in each hand. His cheeks flushed. Tears streamed down his face, and his nose was running.

"Pathetic," Mara said. "Matchstick is a pathetic crybaby. Let's go." The others didn't look at him. They followed her lead and walked away.

Connor watched them go with so much rage and anger burning in his heart that he *felt* like a matchstick. He felt like he could set the entire world on fire.

CHAPTER 18

Twilight in Alaska seemed to go on forever. The sun had fallen below the horizon, but it was like we'd been stuck in an in-between stage ever since I'd found the headstone with my name on it. It wasn't day and it wasn't night. Everything was gray and soft around the edges. But, as I drove the winding roads leading to the research facility, it seemed that darkness was winning.

Sure, I'd figured out how to steer and give the truck gas, and how to brake when I needed to slow down. What I hadn't figured out was how to turn on the headlights. And in the waning light, it was becoming dangerously difficult to see.

While straining my eyes, I noticed too late that there was a shadowy figure standing in the middle of the road. I slammed on the brakes, but the truck wouldn't stop. *Oh no*, I'd hit a sheet of ice. By then, I could see the creature was a caribou with long, boney antlers. The truck was careening straight for it. I jerked the wheel to the left, sending the vehicle into a tailspin. As the truck spun circles and I got a blurry view of the world passing by, there was nothing I could do. I'd lost all control.

I braced for impact, but it never came. When the truck finally skidded to a stop, the caribou was gone. I thanked God I hadn't hit it, and that everything had stopped spinning. I took a moment to catch my breath and to relish the stillness. Then I went through every switch on the panel until the headlights flicked on. The students wanted me dead, but I didn't have to make it easy for them.

When I found the nerve to press on the gas again, I took it slow. Five minutes later, I turned into the research facility. Since it was a Saturday, Mom's car was the only vehicle in the small parking lot. The sky had grown a dark charcoal gray and with each passing minute, I knew I was creeping closer to the date engraved beneath my name on the thirteenth headstone.

I cut the engine and left the keys dangling in the ignition. Then I went straight for the front doors. My stomach roiled as I limped past the security post and thought of Harold plummeting down the side of the embankment.

Once inside, I screamed at the top of my lungs for my mom. I didn't stop screaming until I heard her voice echoing from down the hall. "Lucy?"

Mom stepped into view like an apparition in her white lab

coat. In fact, for a moment, I feared it wasn't really her. It was hard to tell the difference between what was real and what wasn't anymore. "Mom?"

Thankfully, the expression on her face was one that only she could give. It was all at once warm and scrutinizing. I rushed to her arms, and she wrapped me up in a hug. "Honey, what's wrong? Why are you limping? Where's Harold?"

I choked on all the emotions rising in my throat. I couldn't speak, so I shook my head. Mom frowned while taking a step back to study my face. "How did you get here?" she pressed. "Lucy, talk to me. What's going on?"

I took a deep breath, then said, "Harold is gone."

"Gone? You mean Harold dropped you off and left?"

"No, I mean *gone* gone. I drove myself here." I struggled to find the words to make her understand. "He slipped and fell into the river. Or he might've been pushed. I'm not sure."

She inhaled sharply.

"And I'm . . . I'm in danger, too," I stammered. "The students from my class . . . they're trying to kill me."

Mom's eyes narrowed. "What are you saying?"

"I found my name on a headstone in the graveyard by the school," I said. "The thirteenth headstone. The other students, all twelve of them, are buried there, but not Connor. He escaped somehow, which is why they want me to take his place."

The expression on her face hardened. "This isn't funny," she said. "I know I've been busy with work, but you don't need to make up stories to get my attention."

"That's not it!" I protested.

"I don't understand. You've always been a sensible child. Now this—it isn't like you. If you're being bullied again, just tell me. We'll find a solution."

I was being bullied, but it was so much worse than Mom realized. It was literally life or death. "They started a fire at home," I said, "and they made all the electronics in the house go berserk. It's happening here, too, isn't it? The strange readings—it's all connected. It's all *them*."

The crease lines on my mother's forehead deepened. "Oh, Lucy," she said, clearly exasperated.

"There must be something we can do," I went on. "Please? I think they feed off energy. Can't you shut down the power grid or something?"

"Stop."

"I'm not lying."

"Really, Luce? I can't do this here. Just give me a minute. I'll grab my stuff and I'll take you home. We can continue this conversation there."

I followed Mom out of the hallway and into her office. While she gathered printouts that had been scattered across one of the tables, she kept talking. "I'm sorry. I know the past few days have been rough for you, and I haven't been around. I promise I'll take you to school on Monday. I'll talk to your teacher. It's always hard to be the new kid, but it'll get better."

"You don't get it! It won't get better!" I cried, holding back nothing as I tried to get my point across. "I'll be dead!"

I was about to explain how they'd attempted everything from smashing me with a falling tree limb to electrocution so far, and that I wasn't sure how they would kill me, but that it was going to happen, when she looked me dead in the eye and said, "That is enough." Mom's words sliced right through me. It wasn't so much what she said, but how she said it. She'd never spoken to me with so much ice-cold fury in her voice.

I took a step back. My entire life, I'd looked up to her, but now she wasn't the person I needed her to be. No matter what I said, she wouldn't believe me. *Couldn't* believe me. She'd never accept that anything paranormal was real.

But I knew if I went home now, Mara and the others would make sure I didn't live past tomorrow. I had to do something, and I had to do it here and now, before we left. Whenever the students terrorized me, they drained power from the research facility. It was why the readings had driven Mom crazy. She couldn't find an explanation for what was causing the strain on the power grid, but I knew. Mara and the others had been using the electricity all along for online classes. But recently, they'd grown greedy. They were siphoning more and more power.

The research facility had originally been the main power plant for White Pine. It still housed a giant turbine, generator, and a transmission station. The central building had been expanded, however, and labs were added when it was discovered that the phantomium could be used to produce energy here.

I didn't know exactly how the students were harvesting the energy. I just knew in my gut that they were. And when Ciara had given me a tour of the facility, she'd pointed out the computer mainframe that controlled the generator. If I could destroy it, maybe I could cut the students off. My best hope for survival was that if the facility was powerless, they would be, too.

Before I knew what I was doing, I took another step backward and then another, until I was all the way out of the office.

Mom glanced up. She tilted her head questioningly while staring at me through the open doorway. "Where are you going?"

I gave Mom a weak smile, then took off hobbling down the hallway. I could hear the patter of her footsteps behind me. "Lucy!" Mom called sharply. "Get back here!"

My sprained ankle had improved some since I'd swan-dived out of Harold's truck, but it was still tender and slowed me down. By the time I reached the room with the computer main-frame, Mom was right on my heels. She followed me inside.

Ignoring her, I scanned the rows of giant cabinets brimming with electronics. So many lights and buttons! It was overwhelming, and I didn't know where to begin turning off the system. If only Ciara had also pointed out the power switch, or better yet, an ax or baseball bat.

"What's going on?" Mom asked. "Why won't you answer me?"

I was tempted to try once more to get through to Mom, but then the door swung shut and there was a loud CLICK. Mom spun around and immediately jiggled the door handle. "It's locked," she said, her voice laden with disbelief.

I swallowed the bile rising in my throat. "They're here," I whispered.

She peered through the glass panel. "I don't see anyone. The locks are electronic, and Harold and I are the only ones who know the code." She turned to face me. Half smiling, half smirking, she said, "Oh, I get it. The two of you planned this. Well, you got me." She retrieved a radio clipped to the pocket of her lab coat and pressed a button. "Very funny, Harold," she droned. "Now unlock the doors."

There was only static at first, then a cackle followed by a girl's voice. "I'm afraid Harold can't help you right now. Or ever again, for that matter."

Mom scowled at the radio. "Who is this?" she demanded. "This is a private channel."

The sound of Mara's laughter sent slivers of ice down my spine. *This is bad.* We were trapped and Mara was in control. Instinctively, I backed away from the cackles emitting from the radio. The noise seemed to be sucking all the air out of the room.

"We're Lucy's friends," Mara said. "We very much want her to join us, but we know she's anxious. It's so difficult to be the only new student."

Another voice joined in, "Right, so we're coming for her."

"What Jamie means is: 'we're coming *to* her,'" Mara corrected. "We'll see you soon."

Mom frowned at the radio when it went silent. "I'll admit, your new classmates are a bit much," she said. "I wonder how they got access to this channel. On Monday I'll ask your teacher to speak with their parents. I'm sure—"

Mom's eyes suddenly went wide, and she lunged forward. "Look out!"

My gaze shot up to see that one of the largest cabinets, one that went from the floor to the ceiling, was rocking and tipping over. It was going to land right on top of me! I flung my hands up to cover my head just as Mom jumped between me and the heavy metal frame. I was slammed to the floor, while Mom landed on top of me, and the cabinet on top of her.

With the brunt of the cabinet's weight being held up by my mom's hips and shoulders, I was able to wiggle free. Mom, on the other hand, had gone frighteningly still. My heart felt like a brick in my chest. She had shielded me from the blow and taken it herself. With every shred of strength I could muster, I attempted to lift the cabinet. But it was way too heavy. I tried again, but it still wouldn't budge. I knelt beside her. "Mom!" I said, and gently shook her shoulder. Tenderly brushing back a strand of her wavy brown hair, I whimpered. "Oh, Mom." Then I pressed my face close to her mouth. When warm breath wafted across my cheek, I was overcome with relief. Still, I knew we were far from being safe.

I glanced at the analog clock hanging above the door. The day and evening had slipped away. Both hands pointed straight up. It was midnight. That meant it was April 13, the day I was going to die. It was here. There wouldn't be any more running. It was too late.

A loud POP drew my attention away from the clock to a nearby electrical cabinet. It crackled again and then smoke began rising from the panel. A second later the entire cabinet burst into flame. So, this was it. Mom was incapacitated, the door was locked, and now there was a fire. Each time my life had been threatened before, they'd only been toying with me. This was where Mara and the others had wanted me all along.

As hopeless as my situation seemed, though, I didn't plan to go down without a fight. I stood up and scanned the room, looking for something to douse the flames. It was then that I felt the familiar sensation of being watched. My skin crawled. "Connor? I know you're there, Connor!" I screamed. "Help us, please!" Here I was calling on a ghost for assistance. I was calling to the thirteenth child. Why would he put himself back into the very position he'd once managed to escape? Maybe this was exactly where he wanted me, too.

CHAPTER 19

CONNOR
APRIL 13, 1925

The morning after his fishing rod was broken, Connor had trouble getting out of bed. When his baby brother cried for milk, Connor pulled the sheepskin blanket over his head. He neglected his chores. He hid from the world until his mother came to check on him.

His mother was loving but stern. He rarely lied to her, but when he'd come home empty-handed, Connor told her the fish weren't biting. He still couldn't bring himself to tell her about the bamboo pole. After finding his temperature to be normal and proclaiming that what ailed him was "just a wee bit of spring fever," she sent him on his way. It wasn't so much spring fever that was holding him back from school as it was a wounded heart.

The look on Mara's sneering face as she broke his Christmas present in two was forever seared in his brain. Was he supposed to go to school and pretend it never happened?

With no fish to fry, his mother had made a pot of beans and a dried apple pie for dinner the night before. Connor had barely touched his food. Today his belly felt hollow, but he still couldn't bring himself to eat. He picked at the bacon and biscuits she'd served for breakfast. He approached the long walk to school with no more stamina than he had his past two meals. Without a doubt, it would be the dunce hat and the corner for him that day. Ms. Grant wasn't one to overlook tardiness. Of course, now that he was late, would it really matter how much time he took to get there? The punishment would be the same either way. Connor took a detour by the river.

He skipped rocks, angrily whipping them toward the water. With each stone, he wished terrible things to befall the other students. Boils and illnesses, slivers beneath their fingernails. It took a great many throws, but eventually his anger waned. Enough, at least, that he felt he could face going to school.

Connor saw the plume of smoke rising above the tree line before he saw the schoolhouse. It didn't immediately strike him as odd. April mornings were frigid, and Ms. Grant would have lit a fire upon her arrival. He hadn't forgotten about finishing his job of cleaning the chimney, but it seemed of little importance now. He would get around to it at some point, as well as the chores he'd neglected at home that morning. Connor wasn't one to shirk from his duties. In fact, he might even complete the sweep today. It never crossed his mind that his unfinished work could have grave consequences.

As the school came fully into view, so did the flames that were engulfing the roof. The sight was stunning. Connor could do nothing more than stop and stare at the brilliant blaze of orange and red licking the cobalt-blue sky. Through the window, he could see Ms. Grant carrying out a lesson as she stood near the chalkboard. She seemed no more aware of the fire than the pupils sitting attentively in their seats.

Connor thought to call out a warning, but he couldn't find his voice quickly enough. In a frightful instant, the area of roof directly above the doorway collapsed. With it fell a heavy wooden beam consumed by flames, blocking the only entrance to the one-room schoolhouse.

Connor sprang into action, only to find himself helplessly circling the building. Not only was the entrance blocked, but the windows were also barred to protect the glass from the harsh winter conditions. He ran to one of the windows. Bracing his feet against the brick building, he yanked on the crisscrossing sections of metal rods, but he was small and frail, and the rods were bolted down.

Clearly, the fire had started on the roof, not inside the building. It hadn't been struck by lightning—there wasn't a cloud in the sky. No, the buildup of soot and tar from the chimney had burst into flames. The buildup that wouldn't have been there if he'd finished cleaning the flue. Connor stumbled backward. *This was his fault.*

The students were screaming now, and there was nothing he could do. He couldn't bear to stand there and watch them suffer, so, he ran. He ran and ran, and he didn't stop until he was deep in the wilderness.

His lungs burned and his body ached when he stopped. He was far from the schoolhouse, but the students' screams still echoed in his ears. It occurred to him that if he hadn't stopped to throw stones in the river, he would've been with the others when the fire started. Worse, he felt like he'd somehow wished this upon them. He'd been so angry with them, and hadn't he wished for wicked and terrible things? Was the fire a manifestation of his darkest desires?

The guilt piled up on him as he continued to question his actions. Why hadn't he looked for an ax to break through the flaming beam? Why hadn't he gone for help instead of running away? A tiny, blackened corner of his heart whispered that they had gotten what they deserved. Connor choked and retched at the thought. If he'd eaten more than a few bites of breakfast, he would have spilled the contents of his stomach.

For a while after that, Connor tried to block all thoughts from his mind. He wandered aimlessly. It wasn't his intention to spend the night outdoors, but he couldn't bring himself to go home. There was little shelter to be found, and so he walked until he was too tired to go on. When he did lie down, he shivered uncontrollably and grew so cold that his fingers and toes tingled and burned before going numb.

The terrible thoughts crept back in. When the news of the fire reached his family, he knew they would think him dead. Maybe that was for the best. If everyone believed he perished along with the other students, it would save his family the horror of knowing it was their son's fault.

Plus, White Pine was so very tiny, every family would be affected by this. If they knew Connor was responsible, they would shun his parents. The people here depended on one another for survival. And this was so much worse than a dispute over property boundaries or stolen livestock. If the other families refused to trade crops, or denied their services in any number of ways, what would become of his family? Connor knew they would starve.

Connor was so very cold, and his thoughts were sluggish. His wool coat wasn't enough to keep him safe from the frigid air. Even if he had something with which to start a fire, he wasn't sure he could. The temperature would soon drop well below zero. He knew it unlikely that he would survive the night, but he couldn't go back. Not ever. His shame had to remain a secret. As awful and heavy as it was, he would carry it with him forever.

CHAPTER 20

CONNOR
APRIL 13, 2025

It was happening again. After giving the keys to the girl, he'd told himself to stay away. Why hadn't he listened?

Connor had one advantage over the others. He had died cold and alone, but he'd died a wanderer. The twelve had each other in their final moments, but they'd all been trapped. For that reason, they had limited ability to roam the earth while he was freer to come and go as he pleased. Over time, he'd learned that their reach didn't extend much past the tiny graveyard, or the electrical lines in which they found passage. With this knowledge, Connor had managed to avoid their presence for a hundred years.

He could avoid them still. In fact, if he let them take the girl, they might find rest at last. They might stop looking for him. Wasn't that what they wanted? Wasn't it what he wanted, too?

Mr. Johnstone, the baker, had been the first from town to discover that White Pine Secondary was burning. He opened his bakery each morning before dawn. He closed it around the same time that school let out each day. A menacing black cloud and orange glow had drawn him from the main road to investigate. When he arrived at the schoolhouse, he'd found an unresponsive Ms. Grant just inside the door. Unable to reach the others, he'd found a way to drag her out from beneath the beam. She was still breathing. The town doctor did all he could, but she'd inhaled too much smoke, and she passed the next morning.

As Connor had imagined would happen, he was presumed to have died with the rest of the students. The families of White Pine mourned their children greatly. They hurried to order their headstones and dig thirteen graves.

Connor knew all this because, after he'd gone to sleep in the forest never to wake up, his spirit had lingered. He watched and he listened, and he hid, for an entire century. No living soul knew of his detour that day, or that it was his fault the fire ignited in the chimney and spread to the roof. But the twelve knew, and they had also lingered. He could feel them in the breezes and in the currents.

They were there when the townsfolk sifted through the ruins. They were there when the bones were recovered.

There were whispers and accusations, but no answers. At least none that the townsfolk could hear. So, thirteen headstones remained in the tiny graveyard, despite there being only enough remains to fill twelve graves.

It was decades later when electricity finally came to White Pine. Mara and the others had been buried in the soil near the schoolhouse. Soil that held a rare mineral with the ability to conduct a charge. At some point, there was a buildup of particles and a spark, and at last, they found a way to communicate with the living. By then, however, most of their families had buried their pain and moved away. But the students couldn't move on. Over the years, their bitterness grew, as did their desire to fill the empty grave.

And now they'd caught their prey. They had the girl and her mother trapped, and Connor was watching. Could he just ignore the girl's screams and walk away, leaving her and the flames behind? He had done it once before. Repeating this fate over and over seemed to be his lot in life, and in death, too, apparently. He was cursed to bear witness to the suffering of others. Or would this finally put an end to the cycle? If they took the girl, would that be enough? Would the nightmare finally be over? But what if taking her life didn't satisfy their hunger? Not to mention that Lucy was innocent.

No, he couldn't just watch. Not again. Even if it meant being tormented for all eternity, he wouldn't stand by this time, and he wouldn't run. He could feel the current of energy the others were flowing through. It was right in front of him. Connor steeled himself and then stepped into it.

CHAPTER 21

I heard the click of the door unlocking and turned my head to see Connor standing in the doorway. "We have to hurry," he said.

"My mom." I gestured to her. "Please. We can't leave her."

He was beside me in an instant. When we were both in position, I counted, "One, two, three." Then, with our hands cradling opposite ends of the cabinet, we lifted and heaved at the same time. As soon as she was in the clear, I pulled Mom safely aside. Not even a second later, the lights started flashing and the blaring sound of an alarm filled the room.

Connor caught my gaze in the strobing lights. "Take your mom and go," he said. "Maybe they'll leave you alone if they have me."

I knew I should do as he said. This wasn't my debt to pay. I hadn't been there a hundred years ago, and none of this was my fault. Connor had admitted he was to blame, and he was already dead. What more could they do to him? Then the sound of

Mara's laughter filled my ears, and I knew they could do a lot more. Despite my fears, I knew that I couldn't just leave Connor behind.

"Go," he said again, but before I could but before I could reply, the lights blinked off and back on, and then they were there— all twelve students crowded in between us and the door. They appeared as I had seen them online for the past six months. Their clothes were neatly pressed and there wasn't a scar or burn on any of them.

"No one is going anywhere," Mara said in a falsely sweet voice. She seemed to notice me staring and added, "You're wondering why we look different now. When you saw us the first time in real life, we looked an absolute fright, didn't we?"

I swallowed. Stumbling backward, I bumped into another electrical cabinet. Out of the corner of my eye, I could see a number of dials and switches. If only Mom would wake up, I could ask her which one turned off the generator.

Jamie piped in. "We're stronger now, and we'll keep growing stronger."

"You feed off the energy from this facility," I said. "You're like leeches, or parasites."

Mara smiled wickedly in return. "Indeed." The lights in the cabinets and on the electrical panels flickered and danced in response.

"Please," I pleaded. "Don't do this." My gaze traveled around the room. I hoped to garner an ounce of sympathy from at least one of them. But even Josephine's round face and large eyes projected a viciously gleeful expression. Whatever kindness or goodness that had existed in each of them when they were living had been sucked dry by their years of hatred and bitterness.

My lungs rejected the smoke growing thicker around me, causing me to cough and choke. The orange of the flames was reflected in Mara's eyes. She smirked again."Good," she said, clearly pleased to see me struggle. Her eyes went to Connor next, and I thought I caught a flash of anger mixed with disappointment. It hit me then that they didn't just want to fill the empty grave. They were hungry to watch someone suffer the way they had. Connor would no longer satisfy their cravings. They wanted someone living. They were here to watch me perish in the fire.

Before, when they'd been at my cabin, I'd been able to push past them when the lights went out, because I'd timed my escape for a moment when they were weaker. Not only were they draining the electricity, but they were also affected by the surges. It was like a game of tug-of-war. Back and forth. Their energy came in waves and pulses, depending on how much they could pull from the system.

They were strong now, drawing a constant stream of power from the facility. I knew I wouldn't be able to get past them to the unlocked door this time. There was something else I hadn't considered. Even if I found the off switch, it wasn't reasonable to think that White Pine could be cut off from electricity forever. Shutting down the generator might work, but only for a little while. Only until Mara found another spark of energy to play with. Then what? I suspected that the students could fill the thirteenth grave a million times over and still not be satisfied.

Another thing occurred to me. I knew enough about electronics to know that if they were turned off, they could also be turned back on. If they were shorted out, however . . . well, sometimes, they were ruined. I cast a furtive glance at the dials once more. If I could create a strong enough surge, maybe the energy would be too much for the students to handle. Maybe they could be "shorted out." It was a long shot, but it was all I had.

In the fraction of a second it took me to formulate a plan, I caught Connor's attention. I still didn't know why he hadn't died in the fire with the others, but I no longer questioned his intentions. What I did question was what would become of him if I managed to create a dangerous power surge.

I mouthed the words, "You go."

His eyes grew wide, and his lips silently formed the word "no" in return.

I nodded at the dials, willing him to understand. Then I said aloud this time, "GO, NOW!"

He cast me a grave look before disappearing in an instant. Connor's sudden departure was enough to buy me a moment's distraction. I dove for the electrical panels and spun every dial I could find to the right.

"What are you doing?" Mara hissed.

A sizzling noise came from above my head and a live wire snaked toward me. I dodged the sparking wire, then hurried to the next panel and turned up the voltage on those dials as well.

"Stop!" The rage in Mara's voice was laced with fear.

I chanced a glance at the students. The scars and wounds and singed clothing had reappeared. The twelve shimmered a little now, too, like they were a reflection instead of standing there in the room. I kept spinning dials as fast as I could reach them.

Peter and Jamie lunged at me. They grabbed and then restrained my arms. Where their hands touched my clothing, it felt like hot coals. My eyes stung from all the smoke. I coughed and choked some more as I fought against them, but I couldn't break free. They were too strong.

Yet, little by little, their hold on me weakened. It *was* working. The power flow was more than they could handle.

I summoned all my strength at once and pulled away. I spun another dial, and then another. When I dared to look, I saw light radiating from the students' mouths and eye sockets. Then, there was a sudden, blinding flash. It was so bright, I was forced to look away.

When I opened my eyes, they were gone.

"Lucy?" Mom's woozy voice drew my attention. I dropped down beside her. Her eyelids fluttered open. She was starting to come around!

Despite the vanishing of Mara and the others, if Mom hadn't regained consciousness, there was I good chance I wouldn't be able to get her out alive. The smoke was so thick now, I could hardly see through it. Plus, we were deep inside the building. There was no way I could've carried Mom all the way to safety, even if my ankle wasn't sprained.

Fortunately, she was with it enough for me to help her to her feet and lead her outdoors, but she was far from acting like herself. I used her phone to call for help. The closest fire service was in Fairbanks, which meant we would have to wait over an hour for them to arrive. I found some tarps and an old blanket in the back of Harold's truck. Spreading them on the ground a safe distance from the burning building, I tried to make Mom as comfortable as possible. She'd taken a nasty blow to the head and seemed confused about everything. No doubt, she was even more confused when a boy with brilliant red hair appeared out of nowhere.

I sprang to my feet and quickly limped toward him. "Connor!" The boy smiled shyly as I threw my arms around him. "I didn't know. I thought . . . the surge . . ." I stammered, not knowing what to say. I settled on, "I was afraid you might've been caught in it, too."

He shook his head. "No. I didn't want to leave you, but I'm good at running away." The sadness in his voice caught me off guard.

"Were they cruel to you, too? I mean, when you went to school with them . . . back before the fire, did they treat you badly?"

Connor nodded. "And I ran. When the school was burning, I didn't help them."

"But you came when I needed you," I said. "We couldn't have gotten out if you hadn't unlocked the doors."

Connor smiled wistfully. "Thank you," he said, then added, "I think it's time for me to go."

I didn't know what to say to that, so I said, "I didn't have a chance to sew you a pouch, for your fishing gear."

"But you offered. That meant a great deal."

"Friends?" I asked.

"Friends." Connor's smile turned apologetic. "I really should go . . . I can hear my mother. She's calling me. It's been so long since I've heard her voice, and I want to go home."

I smiled, too, then mouthed, "Go."

And he did.

AFTER

I studied my appearance in the mirror and smiled. I was wearing a T-shirt and a floral skirt I'd sewn on my grandmother's sewing machine. The machine had operated perfectly since we'd returned to San Francisco. First days still made me nervous, though. It had been four months since the incident, and three months since we'd moved back to California. The day after the research facility had burned to the ground, Dad made the trip back to Alaska and met us in Fairbanks where Mom had been taken for treatment. Surprising to Dad, but not to me, the computer issues he'd been having with Seas the Day's internal server cleared up around the same time as the fire.

We only returned to our cabin once, the day after Mom was discharged from the hospital in Fairbanks. The power grid in White Pine was out indefinitely, and my parents said our home was "uninhabitable" without a reliable heat source. While they tied up loose ends and prepared for the moving company, I wandered outside. There was something I had to do.

I carried my fabric scissors and a folded step stool to the place where the gull was still strung from the tree. Its flesh had decayed, and all that remained dangling from the fishing line were soiled feathers and a fragile skeleton.

I used the scissors to snip the fishing line, then carried the bones with me as I walked back through the woods. While I went, I paid attention to my senses, trying to tell if the forest still felt like it had eyes. It didn't, and that made me happy. Just to be sure, I called out Connor's name. He didn't respond.

Whatever had been holding him here, I knew he'd been released. He was finally free. When I got back to the cabin, I buried the bird's skeleton in the backyard, directly below my window. Mom found me as I was shoveling on the last bit of dirt. "What are you doing?"

Neither of my parents really understood what had happened. Other than Connor, Mom had never seen any of the White Pine Secondary students. And she'd been concussed when he'd appeared. Mom and Dad believed Harold was responsible for everything. They thought he'd been the one to sabotage the research facility, and that he'd done it before picking me up at the cabin that day. Everyone agreed I'd been lucky to get away.

No one wanted to imagine what could have happened to me if he hadn't fallen in the river.

Any time I tried to point out any supernatural occurrences, they said I'd "been through a lot" and that "attributing fear and distress to the unknown is normal after trauma."

I stood and turned to face my mother. Her head was still wrapped in a bandage. Her voice, the way she stood, her eyes, everything about her seemed tired and vulnerable. I didn't want to answer her question—I didn't want to bring up anything else involving death. But I also didn't want to lie. "I was burying a dead bird."

"I see," she said quietly. After a short pause she added, "I never thanked you for saving my life, and I'm sorry for my behavior this past week. I was so dismissive and unavailable when you needed me."

That was true, but she seemed more present now. I considered taking her by the hand and leading her to the ruins and then the tiny graveyard. It would've been my best shot at convincing her that it was all real. "Mom—" I started, then cut myself off. She had been through a lot, too. I'd never thought of her as fragile, but she was in a way. She'd spent the morning on the phone making arrangements for Ciara and the other employees who were affected by the fire. I knew she did it because she was a caring person, but I could tell she was also clinging to structure and doing what was practical as she made her lists and checked off boxes. It was how she would get through this, and I didn't want to be the one to shatter her ordered world with something that would upend the way she saw everything.

"Yes?" she prompted me to continue.

"Nothing . . . Just, I love you."

Her face lit up. "I love you, too," she said, and I knew letting it go was the right decision.

When we returned to California, we moved even closer to Cesar Chavez Middle, close enough for me to ride my skateboard to and from school. Mom joined the faculty at the university where she'd earned her PhD and would be teaching grad students while continuing her research on renewable energy sources. I was just glad phantomium wasn't a mineral that could be found anywhere near San Francisco. Dad kept his beard and grizzly northern style (along with the board shorts he'd never given up) and happily returned to running the surf shop each day.

Now, on the first day of seventh grade, I rolled up to Cesar Chavez Middle, then dismounted before flipping my skateboard into my hands. I tucked it under one arm and took a deep breath while entering the building. It had been nearly a year, but many of the faces were familiar. Luckily, as far as I knew, none of them would be trying to lure me to an early grave this year.

Almost immediately, Hana Lee was there by my side. I'd seen Hana multiple times since returning to California, and we'd spent the last few glorious days of summer going back and forth between Seas the Day and the Lee family's gift shop next door. Turns out, Hana had never stopped texting me. The only thing I could figure was that Mara had found a way to intercept the messages. Walking down the hall with my best friend made the last of my jitters disappear.

With Hana being a year ahead of me and starting eighth grade this year, we had different schedules, but our first period classes were right next door to each other. "Want me to show you where Honors History is?" Hana asked.

I nodded, then raised my skateboard. "I just need to drop this off at my locker first."

Locker #107 was right down the hall. Opening the latch was a cinch, and I had a feeling that it was going to be a great first day. That was until my phone dinged and I slid it out of my pocket to check the message. I'd cleared my entire contact list from White Pine, so the text came from an unknown number. Still, I knew without a doubt who'd sent it. My blood turned to ice as I read: *We're going to have so much fun.*

ABOUT THE AUTHOR

Jenny Goebel is the author of *Grave Images*, The 39 Clues: *Mission Hurricane*, *Fortune Falls*, *Out of My Shell*, *Alpaca My Bags*, *Backcountry*, and *Pigture Perfect*. She lives in Denver with her husband and three sons. She can be found online at jennygoebel.com.